A sudden, vicious gust of wind sprayed Susannah's exposed face with pellets of frozen rain. She pulled her hood up over her still-damp ponytail, ducked her head down, and walking as carefully as she could, made her way down the wide, stone steps and over to the car.

When she reached the Benz, she threw herself into it with relief, but the secure feeling lasted only until she started down the hill. The frozen precipitation was coming faster now, and sticking. Susannah had barely left the crest of the hill when the car began to slide sickeningly to the left. Though she fought the wheel, struggling for control, the car continued to aim straight for the drop-off into dark nothingness.

Med Center

Virus

Flood

Fire

Blast

Blizzard

Poison

MED CENTER

DIANE HOH

SCHOLASTIC INC.
New York Toronto London Auckland Sydney

ISBN 0-590-89754-3

12 11 10 9 8 7 6 5 4 3 2 1   6 7 8 9/9 0 1/0

Printed in the U.S.A.   01

First Scholastic printing, January 1997

prologue

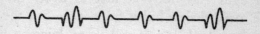

It began as rain. Not a warm, gentle shower, but a steady, chilly downpour that drenched streets and buildings and people unlucky enough to get caught in it. As the day progressed, temperatures plummeted. The rain began to freeze on its way down, turning to tiny ice pebbles that bounced off sidewalks and made sharp pinging sounds as they hit car hoods and metal drainpipes and tin roofs.

As darkness fell, every exposed surface in the city of Grant, Massachusetts, glittered with the thin, treacherous coating of ice. "Black ice," it was called, because it was difficult to see until you found your car or your feet or your bicycle wheels sliding across it out of control. Drivers cried out in terror as their vehicles spun wildly into one another. The air echoed with the sound of metal crunching against metal. Ambulances on their way to rescue accident victims found themselves fender-to-fender with other ambulances. Under the weight of the ice, power lines snapped, hissing and crackling their way to the frozen ground.

When the city had become entirely coated with the deadly sheath of ice, snow began to fall. The rapidly thickening overcoat of white, too light and fluffy at first to make the ice safe, nevertheless hid it from view. But the ice hadn't melted. It was still there, lying in wait for its next victims.

A deceptively beautiful disguise, the snow continued to fall.

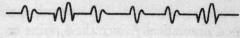

In spite of the noisy whirring of her blow-dryer, there was no mistaking the sudden pleasant drumming of rain on the roof of Linden Hall. Susannah Grant switched off the hair-dryer and, tilting her head, listened. Pinging on the roof. Pinging against the windows. Pinging on the hoods of cars parked below. Freezing rain, Susannah thought. She sighed. How was she going to get back down the steep, curving hill if it was slick with ice?

Three hours earlier, when she'd left the private day school she attended, it had begun raining as she drove her silver Mercedes convertible along Linden Boulevard.

"Isn't it awfully cold to be raining?" Abby O'Connor asked. Abby, Susannah's closest friend, was nestled in the passenger's seat. Shorter than Susannah and rounder, with short, dark curly hair and dark eyes, Abby wore over her blue-and-white cheerleader's uniform a full-length black hooded cape she'd bought at a thrift shop. "Maybe it'll make me look mysterious," she'd said jokingly to Susannah as she paid for it. It didn't. Abby's round, pretty face was too open and honest to denote mystery. But Susannah wished she had on a coat as warm as Abby's, instead of her thin blue windbreaker. The temperature had dropped dramatically since she'd put it on that morning.

Abby attended Grant High, but Susannah usually picked her up for the ride home. Or to Med Center if they had volunteer shifts immediately after school. They weren't due there on this Friday until seven P.M. "It was so warm yesterday," Abby had added, "I just wore a sweater to school. I can't believe it's getting so cold. Shouldn't it be snowing? That'd be nicer. Then we could go skiing one last time before spring gets here."

"It's still not cold enough for snow," Susannah had contradicted. "But it *is* colder than yesterday." Turning on her wipers, she added, "I hope it doesn't get much colder, or the roads will turn into skating rinks." Puddles in the O'Connor driveway splashed as Susannah drove through them. "I'll pick you up at six-thirty, okay? That gives us a couple of hours to shower and change."

After dropping Abby off, Susannah drove up the hill to Linden Hall, the Grant family

4

home. A massive stone and frame structure, it was the only residence occupying the top of the hill. Overlooking the city of Grant like a sentinel, the mansion sometimes reminded Susannah of a castle, though it was modern in design. Still, the idea of a castle seemed appropriate. Everyone knew that if the city of Grant had been ruled by royalty, her parents, Samuel II and Caroline Grant, would absolutely have been king and queen.

Now, dryer still in hand, Susannah hurried to one of the long, narrow windows of her three-room suite on the second floor of Linden Hall. If that pinging sound meant hail, her father would flip out. They never garaged the cars on a Friday afternoon, because they would all be using them again that evening. Her twin brother, Samuel Grant III, would be off to a party or a dance or a game in his sleek, silver van. Her parents would be taking the white Cadillac or the cranberry Jaguar to a party or a dinner or a concert. And Susannah would be steering her silver Mercedes down the hill toward the huge medical complex in the heart of Grant, which she and Abby affectionately called "Emsee."

If that *was* hail she was hearing, every vehicle would be pockmarked within a matter of minutes. Not that her father couldn't afford to replace damaged cars. Of course he could. In a mini-second. But he didn't like to see things ruined. Especially *his* things.

Pressing her face against the cold, rain-streaked glass, Susannah peered out. The outside light was on in the porte cochere. Her father's Cadillac and her mother's Jag were safely parked beneath it. No hail damage there. But the gardener's Jeep and her own Mercedes were parked, unprotected, in the steep, circular driveway.

In the porte cochere's bright light, Susannah could see no sign of hailstones bouncing off the hood or roof of her car. The pinging sound had to be coming from the rain, which was better for the cars, but worse for the roads. Freezing rain could last for hours, and coat the roads and streets with a treacherous layer of ice.

It was Friday night. "Accident night," the staff in the ER, where she did most of her volunteer work, called it. Every staff member would be needed, including any volunteers who were available. And that was *without* bad weather.

If the freezing rain hung around long enough, she'd never get to the hospital.

Turning away from the window, Susannah hastily pulled her long blond hair into a wavy ponytail, donned jeans and a thick, hand-knit sweater, and yanked on a pair of black suede boots. Snatching up her fleece-lined, Sherpa jacket and brown leather shoulder bag from the chair where she'd left them, she hurried out of the suite.

She was on her way to the front door when the sound of her boot heels on the hallway's quarry tile alerted her mother. Caroline Grant, beautifully groomed in suede trousers and a white cashmere sweater, appeared in the doorway of the library, an open book in her hands, a questioning frown on her lovely face. "You can't possibly be thinking of going out, Susannah," she said.

That meant, Susannah knew, that she *shouldn't* be thinking of going out. "It's Friday night. I have volunteer duty at ER."

"Well, yes, I know it's Friday, darling. Your father and I had plans. The symphony. But of course we canceled." Her mother waved a hand toward the door. The huge diamond solitaire on her left ring finger gleamed. "The weather is becoming quite nasty. I understand it's expected to get much worse. Ice, perhaps snow, a blizzard, they're saying."

"I'll make it to Emsee before then." Susannah began moving toward the door again. "If it's really bad, I'll just stay all night at the hospital. I've done it before."

"Susannah."

Reluctantly, Susannah turned around. Her mother's smile was tolerant. It was, at first glance, a kind, loving smile. But it was deceptive. That smile was designed to get Caroline Grant what she wanted. Most often, it worked. "Darling, you're just a volunteer. You don't *have* to be there. Someone else can surely fold towels and wheel those little carts from room to room. Isn't that what they pay orderlies to do?"

Susannah inhaled and tried to count to ten. She hated this attitude of her parents so *much*. The way they thought of her volunteer work as a harmless amusement, something to occupy her time, like her mother's piano playing and bridge games, her father's golfing, her brother's tag football on Saturday afternoons.

It wasn't that they had anything against what her mother called "giving back to the community." Both Caroline and Samuel Grant II were active in volunteer work, and they took it seriously. It was just *Susannah's* volunteer work they didn't take seriously. Partly, she knew, because her parents felt she should be out partying and having a good time, like her twin brother, Sam. They just didn't get it that she and Sam, twins or not, were very different people.

"I do more than fold towels, Mother," Susannah answered coolly. "I'm going to be *needed* at Emsee tonight."

The smile remained in place. "But the roads are going to be so bad, Susannah! And I had Paolo build a lovely fire in the fireplace. Wouldn't it be lovely to laze around tonight, just the two of us, nice and cozy? I could have Mary Margaret make hot chocolate. With marshmallows, the way you like it."

As if she were ten, instead of seventeen. And Mary Margaret, one of their housekeepers, should be on the way to her *own* house before the weather got too bad. She shouldn't be hanging around here waiting to see if the Grants needed hot chocolate. "I hate marshmallows, Mother. They stick to my teeth." Then repentant, she quickly added, "Isn't Dad home? He'll keep you company. Or Sam, if he's home." Doubtful. It would take a lot more than icy roads to keep Sam Grant home on a Friday night.

Caroline's cheeks deepened in color, and she stood up straighter. "Your brother went out five minutes after he got home from school. And your father had an emergency at the refinery. Since we'd already decided not to go to the symphony, he decided to handle the problem himself." Thinly disguised, injured pride sounded in her voice. "But I wasn't looking for

9

company, Susannah." She held up her open book. "I have my novel, one I've been dying to read for weeks, and that lovely fire in the fireplace. You go on, if you think you absolutely have to. But please be careful. Call me when you get to the hospital."

Impulsively, Susannah took a few steps forward to kiss her mother on the cheek. "I'll be fine, Mom. The Benz handles like a dream, you know that. It's no problem."

But when she had shut the front door, the wind hit her. Tiny ice pellets stung her face, her feet slid on the slick porch. She could see a thin, glassy veneer shining on the driveway, reflecting the glow of lights from the house.

The Benz *was* a dream to drive. That car could turn on a dime. But *ice*? She had never driven on ice. And Linden Hill was more than just steep. It curved sharply in two places, with a dramatic, sudden drop-off on the left side during the descent. If she lost control of the car and slid to the left, she could sail off into nothingness.

But this was "accident night" in ER. She'd be needed, whether her parents thought so or not. And Abby was actually looking forward to a stint in ER. Usually, Abby volunteered in rehab or psych, preferring the quieter pace of those buildings. But two "floats," volunteers who, like Abby, moved from one hospital to another in the huge complex, had been felled by a flu, leaving the staff short-handed. Astrid Thompson, head nurse in ER, had asked Susannah if she knew anyone who might be willing to fill in for them.

Susannah had expected Abby to wrinkle her nose and say, "No way! *You* might like all that blood and guts and screaming ambulance stuff, but not me. Get someone else." But she hadn't. Instead, she had thought about it, and then answered, "Sure, why not? I'm not qualified to go into the treatment and trauma rooms like you and Kate. But I can help with other stuff. Sid and I don't have any plans. We're going to a movie Saturday night, but Friday night, he's visiting his family. He's actually driving himself, in one of rehab's specially equipped vans. So I'm free as a bird."

Abby was referring to Sid Costello, her boyfriend. Sid had become a patient in rehab following a fall from the Grant water tower that had left him paralyzed from the waist down. He was doing well, although he still had his dark moments. Susannah liked him, and she especially liked seeing Sid and Abby together. They had a warm, free and easy relationship that Susannah envied, particularly when her *not* so free and easy relationship with Will Jackson, a paramedic at Emsee, was going through rocky times. Like now, for instance.

She didn't envy Sid tonight. His first time driving one of the vans would be enough of a challenge, without bad weather to make it even more difficult. Abby would worry. And with good reason.

A sudden, vicious gust of wind sprayed Susannah's exposed face with pellets of frozen rain. She pulled her hood up over her still-damp ponytail, ducked her head down, and walking as carefully as she could, made her way down the wide, stone steps and over to the car.

When she reached the Benz, she threw herself into it with relief, but the secure feeling lasted only until she started down the hill. The frozen precipitation was coming faster now, and sticking. Susannah had barely left the crest of the hill when the car began to slide sickeningly to the left. Though she fought the wheel, struggling for control, the car continued to aim straight for the drop-off into dark nothingness.

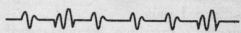

In the year and a half since Susannah's six-teenth birthday when her father had presented her with the Benz, a wide golden ribbon wrapped around it, a basket of flowers the size of a pony perched on the roof, she had driven up or down Linden Hill at least twice a day. Some of those trips had taken place in bad weather. Rain. Snow. A mixture of both. Wind. Some of those trips had even been scary, with that precarious cliff. There *was* a guardrail. But Susannah suspected that if the Benz decided to dive off the edge of the cliff, the guardrail surely wasn't going to stop it.

Those earlier trips, she thought feverishly as she fought to maintain control of the car, were a walk in the park compared to this. The Benz seemed to be in charge, deciding on its own to slide first to the left, then back to the right. Twice the car came within an inch of the guardrail. Only her headlights broke the blackness shrouding the steep, curving hill.

Back and forth, back and forth, the car slid

slowly, crazily, from one side of the road to the other. Susannah hit a curve, and gasped in terror as the car left the road and ran, tilted, along the embankment on her right for several interminable seconds before skidding back onto the road again.

Susannah's breathing became ragged and uneven, her knuckles white from her tense grip on the steering wheel. She had to force herself to keep her foot off the brake. Every instinct in her wanted, needed, to slam down on the pedal, hard, willing the car to stop. But she remembered enough of her driver's ed training to know that would be a terrible mistake, worse even than going out in this stupid weather in the first place.

Her mother had been right. She should have stayed home. She could be sitting by a nice, cozy fireplace now, sipping hot chocolate and reading or watching a video instead of risking her life on this terrifying trip down the treacherous hill.

But . . . Susannah's lips tightened . . . Abby was waiting for her, and so was Emsee. She was *going* to get to Med Center, or die trying.

That is very possible, Susannah, she told herself. Thoroughly frightened, she took a deep breath, sat up straighter, and expertly whipped the steering wheel in the direction of the latest slide toward the edge of the cliff.

And then, as if the car had finally realized that she meant business, it straightened out and followed the curve of the hill the last few hundred feet down to Linden Boulevard.

The street, shining with wetness and lit by tall streetlights, was deserted. It was lined on both sides by huge, stone or frame homes set some distance back from the boulevard, and sheltered by giant, ancient trees. Susannah's friend, Jeremy Barlow, who was currently confined to his room with the same flu that had stricken the nurses at Emsee, lived in this area, as did Callie Matthews, the spoiled, pampered daughter of Caleb Matthews, chief administrator of the eighteen-hospital medical complex that was the core of the city of Grant.

Because Linden Boulevard was more heavily traveled than the hill itself, the ice hadn't had a chance to take hold yet, and Susannah made it to Abby's sprawling ranch house without incident.

On the way, she heard three separate ambulance sirens. No surprise. With weather like this, there would be all kinds of car accidents. Those drivers who were smart enough to wear their safety belts and drive cautiously would suffer only whiplash and minor bruises and lacerations. Those who weren't, and Susannah knew there would be plenty of those, would be brought into Emsee's ER with more serious

15

head injuries, broken bones, and chest wounds from being slammed into the steering wheel.

The roads weren't the only danger. If the freezing rain continued as the night wore on, sidewalks, steps, and porches would be wearing the same thin, slick overcoat. People stepping outside their homes to pick up the evening's newspaper, or take out the garbage, or bring in their plants for the night would slip and fall, breaking an elbow, a hip, a wrist.

Susannah could only hope that whoever had told her mother that a blizzard was on its way had been wrong. Maybe it would warm up again instead, giving them another tantalizing taste of spring. Then Friday night in ER wouldn't be any worse than usual.

But when she got out of the car in the O'Connors' driveway, a vicious blast of wind ripped her hood off her head. She could smell snow in the air, and Susannah decided with some dismay that her mother had probably been right.

As she yanked open the front door to Abby's house, she heard two more sirens wailing in the distance.

Kate Thompson ran from one cubicle to another in Grant Memorial's Emergency Center, pushing a metal cart filled with medical supplies. So far, the injuries had been relatively minor, though there had been some broken bones. People with broken bones did *not* consider their injuries minor.

They'd had a six-year-old boy with a deep laceration over one eye, the result of his attempt to ride his bicycle down an ice-slicked slope. According to Dr. Jonah Izbecki, who was stitching the wound, the boy had been lucky. Another fraction of an inch and he'd have lost all use of the eye. The patient, whose name was Micah, didn't look as if he considered himself lucky, but neither did he shed a tear, not even when the needle pierced his skin.

Four teenagers, none of whom Kate knew, were brought in together, victims of a car wreck caused by a foot too heavily applied to the gas pedal on an icy road. They, too, had been lucky. The most serious injury in the group was a possible concussion the driver had suffered when the car skidded into a stone flood marker at a low-lying intersection. The sudden stop had thrown the young man against the steering wheel. "You should have heard the crack his head made when it hit the wheel," one of his companions told Kate. "Then he went out like a light. We thought he was dead, no kidding."

He wasn't dead. But he *was* going to be kept overnight for observation.

There had been one broken hip and three broken wrists so far, from falls on icy sidewalks or steps or porches. Why didn't people just stay *inside*? Kate wondered irritably. Still, they'd had no codes yet, no life-threatening injuries requiring the extraordinary medical measures that were a part of day-to-day life in ER.

But it was early yet, she reminded herself as she handed a fresh pair of sterile, disposable gloves to Dr. Margaret Mulgrew, the tall, attractive physician who was about to suture a nasty cut on an elderly man's left hand.

"I didn't even *see* the ice," the patient murmured, shaking a thick crop of white hair, "just went out to get the paper, like I always do right before dinner. I didn't know the porch was icy. My feet went right out from under me, and next thing I knew, I was lyin' on my back lookin' up at the porch roof and my hand hurt somethin' fierce. I guess I sliced it on the edge of the snow shovel parked on the porch. Hedda, my wife, she just about went wild when she saw me sprawled out like a dead fish, blood everywhere. She yelled at me, 'Harry Miller, what have you gone and done now, you old fool!' Like I done it on purpose. I told her, I never even *seen* the ice."

Kate moved on with the cart, maneuvering it past orderlies pushing empty gurneys back to treatment and trauma and suture rooms, past nurses assisting patients about to be discharged, past doctors who had been called down from upstairs to consult about a particular patient. The doctors hurried along the corridors fingering the ever-present stethoscopes around their necks. Some of them seldom smiled or called out a greeting.

Someday, she hoped to be one of them. A doctor, with her very own stethoscope dangling around her neck like jewelry. But *she* would say hello to people as she marched through the halls. Having an MD after her name wasn't going to give her a superiority complex. Like Dr. Barlow, Jeremy's father, head of the cardiopulmonary unit. Kate didn't want to be like that. She wanted her patients to feel they could confide in her. Then she could make a better diagnosis, and be a better doctor. She hoped.

So far, the activity in the corridors wasn't unusual enough to alarm Kate. Since she'd passed all of the classes and exams necessary to allow her admittance into the ER trauma and treatment rooms, she could recall very few Friday nights when they hadn't been busy. Still, on this night, with ice pellets rapping on the windows and paramedics arriving with their faces and hands red with cold, their navy blue jackets dripping with melting ice, there was an air of urgency, of anxiety, about the ER that wasn't always there.

Kate found herself wishing Susannah and Abby would arrive soon. It still amazed her that Susannah Grant, daughter of the man whose ancestors had founded the city, the hospital, Grant Pharmaceuticals, the refinery, and the university, was not only unspoiled, but had proved to be a valuable asset to the ER. Susannah was smart, calm in emergencies, and gentle with the patients. When they'd first begun working together, there had been more than one occasion when, during some particularly gruesome procedure, Kate had fully expected Susannah's knees to buckle and send her toppling face first onto the white tile floor.

That hadn't happened. Maybe Susannah's fair skin had gone a shade whiter than usual, but she'd stood her ground and continued to help out. Kate's respect for her had grown with every shift they'd shared. Susannah was a good person to have around when things got hectic.

Abby O'Connor, with her upbeat personality, would be a big help, too. She usually volunteered in rehab or psych. The only reason they were getting her in ER tonight was because Suzie Crater, a "float," had the flu. And even though Abby wouldn't be allowed in the treatment and trauma rooms — of all the high school volunteers, only Kate and Susannah had taken that second step and passed with flying colors — Abby would still be a big help. And she'd probably do a lot to lighten the mood, too, if things got really rough.

Where were they, anyway? Kate glanced up at the huge, round clock high on the wall above the admitting desk. It was seven-thirty-five. They were supposed to clock in at seven. Susannah was always on time. Of course, she wasn't always driving on *ice*. Hoping they hadn't had any trouble on the roads, Kate left the supply cart near the desk, and moved on down the peach-walled corridor to the waiting room, where she could look out the wide window to check on the weather.

It looked much worse out there than it had earlier. She could see the ice glistening on the driveway. How could anyone possibly drive on that?

A tall, slender, dark-skinned girl with perfectly sculpted cheekbones and intelligent brown eyes, Kate turned away from the window. Walking with confidence, her head high, shoulders back, the way her mother had taught her, she returned to ER. The vividly colored, short dashiki she wore in place of the pink volunteer's smock moved gently around her legs.

But the look of confidence was marred

21

somewhat by the concern in her dark eyes. As she walked, she was envisioning the steep, winding curves of Linden Hill. She could see the hill covered with a coat of ice, and she could see Susannah trying valiantly to steer that fancy car of hers downward without sailing out over the edge of the cliff.

What if she hadn't been able to keep the car in check?

Deciding to call Abby's house and see if Susannah had made it safely, Kate headed straight for the phone on the nurses' desk.

Heads often turned when Kate Thompson walked by. Most of the time, she didn't notice. When she *did* notice, she would hide a grin, thinking, Yeah, yeah, so you think I'm pretty, but I'm way more than you can handle. It had been Kate's experience that most men preferred their women to be if not "sweet," then certainly at least "agreeable." And Kate didn't consider herself sweet *or* agreeable. That didn't matter with Damon, though. He seemed to thrive on their disagreements. And it worked out well, since they had so many.

Still, she had to admit that even when he disagreed with her opinions, he never stepped on them. He never cut her off, or told her she was being ridiculous. He just disagreed, openly and emphatically. She was finding, in this new relationship with Damon, that she didn't mind that. As long as he let her say what she needed to say, too. So far, he had.

The waiting room was crowded, which was a little surprising to Kate. It was always crowded on Friday night, but not this early. It wasn't even eight o'clock yet. Friday nights usually peaked after people had been out partying. Then the waiting room filled with their relatives, summoned to ER to pick up the pieces.

Her mother, Head Nurse Astrid Thompson, joined her in the doorway and, borrowing a line from an old movie, murmured, "Fasten your seat belt, honey, it's going to be a bumpy night." She handed Kate a clipboard. "Here, make yourself useful. Find out who hasn't been treated yet and start their charts, okay?"

Kate nodded. "After I call Abby, okay? It'll just take a minute."

Still picturing the winding curves of Linden Hill, glistening and shining slickly with black ice, Kate's stomach felt queasy as she dialed the number.

chapter

3

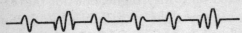

In spite of the weather and the hair-raising drive down Linden Hill, the minute Susannah walked into the O'Connor house, her spirits rose. She could smell chocolate chip cookies baking, and the familiar aroma of lemon furniture polish. Susannah loved walking in the front door. This house was so comfortable, so familiar. She stayed overnight with Abby as often as possible and probably would have done so more often if she hadn't been afraid of hurting her own mother's feelings.

The television set in the living room to her right was on, a blur of bright color. Susannah saw Abby's father Brendan, still recovering from serious burns he'd suffered in a recent refinery fire, sitting on the couch with four-year-old Mattie, the only male child in the family, and Toothless, the baby, a curly haired toddler in pink polka-dot pajamas. Moira, Carmel, and Geneva, Abby's sisters, were sprawled out on the beige carpet, open books on the floor beneath them. Abby's grandfather was asleep in a rocking chair, an afghan on his lap, his feet propped up on a brown fake-leather hassock.

Abby's father's arms were still wrapped in the protective knit coverings he would have to wear until his burns were completely healed. But he looked, at that moment, perfectly content.

Abby rushed into the hallway, her short curls restrained under a bright blue knit cap that matched her ski jacket. "Oh, good, you made it!" she cried breathlessly when she saw Susannah. "Kate just called. She was worried." A look of surprise filled Abby's face. "Can you imagine Kate worried? Her voice was actually *shaking*. She didn't think you could make it down the hill. I'd better run and call her back before we leave, in case it takes us a while to get over there."

When she returned, she said, "Let's see, I've got my purse, my gloves, my boots. Mom! Do you know where my smock is?"

Her mother, Charlie, in jeans and a turtleneck sweater and bare feet in spite of the cold, came down the stairs just then holding out the missing smock. "I've got it. It was in the bathroom. Hi, Sooz. How's the weather out there?" Without waiting for an answer, she added mildly, "And you left your wet towel on the floor again, Abigail dearest."

Abby grinned. "Sorry, mommy dearest. I was in a rush."

"Aren't we all?" Turning to Susannah, Abby's mother asked, "Are you sure it's safe to drive, Susannah? They've been saying on the radio for the past couple of hours that people should be staying home."

"I know. And it *is* nasty out there. If we were going anyplace else, we probably wouldn't go. But I have a feeling ER is going to be wild tonight, and they're going to need all the help they can get. I got down the hill okay, and I figure if I could negotiate that, I shouldn't have too much trouble driving across town on level ground to Emsee, right?"

"We'll be okay, Mom," Abby said, folding the smock and slipping it into her massive shoulder bag. "Don't worry." She grinned. "It'll turn your hair gray." She hurried into the living room to kiss her father good-bye and give good-night hugs to Mattie and Toothless.

"Make her call me when you get there," Charlie told Susannah quietly. "I need to know you're not stranded and turning into ice cubes somewhere between here and Med Center, okay?"

Susannah promised.

In the living room, without turning around, Moira muttered from her place on the floor, "You are *nuts*, going out on a night like this.

You'll end up in a ditch, and then Mom'll have to come and get you."

"You have a nice evening, too, Moira," Abby said cheerfully, and left to return to Susannah.

When they yanked the front door open and another gust of icy wind tore at Susannah's face, clothes, and hair, she thought, I would give anything to stay right here in this nice, warm, cozy house tonight, watching television.

But then she heard another shrill ambulance siren, quickly followed by another, distinctly separate wail.

Pulling her hood back onto her head, she left the porch, leading the way to her car.

Kate glanced around the waiting room. The air reeked with the smell of wet wool. Two patients who had been treated but hadn't been picked up by relatives yet, sat reading magazines. One had his arm in a sling, the other had a white gauze bandage taped to his left cheek.

There were patients still awaiting treatment, most of them holding tissues or gauze over bloody cuts, or wincing as they shifted position, which indicated a sprain or a bad bruise from a fall on the ice. They were watching a television set posted high on an opposite wall, or reading.

There were several coughing, wheezing children sitting beside anxious-looking mothers. Children brought to the ER usually didn't have a regular pediatrician — a clear sign that money was a problem. Kate had heard her mother explaining more than once to a parent that emergency care was more expensive than a visit to a family physician, and that regular, preventive care with a family doctor could ward off more serious problems. But her words usually fell on deaf ears. Those same families showed up repeatedly in ER.

But not, she realized, that family in the corner. Kate had never seen them before. There were two adults and three young children, the oldest, a girl, probably no more than six or seven. The youngest child was on her mother's lap. They were all huddled as close to the radiator as they could get without searing their skin.

No wonder, Kate thought, moving on into the room. Their clothing looked far too thin to be much protection against a frigid night like this. Only the baby seemed to have a hat. A red one. She had yanked it off and was chewing on its knit strap.

Kate made her way around the rows of blue plastic chairs to the family clustered against the wall. When she reached them, she thought she noticed the mother shrinking backward in alarm, but decided that it had to be her imagination. Why would the woman be afraid of a volunteer?

"Okay," Kate said cheerfully, smiling down at the three children, "which one of you is sick?"

"They all are," the mother said hastily. She was thin to the point of boniness, her face still showing some sign of former prettiness. The skin under her eyes was shadowed, her lips dry, her hair in need of a comb and possibly a shampoo. "We think maybe it's the flu. It's going around, you know."

"Are they feverish?" Kate asked, gently laying a hand on the forehead of the middle child. His skin felt dry and cool. No temperature at all, but he was shivering. His dark green jacket looked to be unlined. When Kate touched him, he shrank back as his mother had, and tried to put his hands in his pockets. One pocket was ripped, providing no protection. He didn't seem to know what to do with the hand then, and waved it about helplessly until his mother took it in one of hers. "He feels cool," Kate said. "Has he been throwing up or coughing?"

As if on cue, the oldest child began coughing. The spasms were clearly fake. She politely covered her mouth with one hand. She was a pretty girl, with huge, dark eyes, faintly shadowed. Her thin face was very pale, but her cheeks began to redden as she continued to force the coughing, and the added color gave her a healthier look.

"That's enough, Annie," her father said.

The girl, looking relieved, stopped coughing.

Kate extended the clipboard and a pencil. "I'll need your names, address, and your medical histories, also the dates of the children's inoculations. We'll get to you as soon as we can. We're always pretty busy when the weather is so bad." Glancing at the father's worn, denim jacket, she added as tactfully as she could, "You must have been pretty cold out there. I guess you didn't realize the temperature was going to drop so drastically."

The father sat up very straight, his jaw tightening. "No, no, we didn't know it was going to get so cold," he said stiffly. "Didn't have the TV on all day, and hadn't read the paper yet."

"And we'd already put their winter jackets away," the mother joined in. "I mean, it was so warm earlier this week, remember? So I just stuck all our winter stuff away and like Jake says," she said, glancing nervously at her husband and at the same time clutching the child closer to her chest, "we just didn't know it was going to get nasty again. As soon as the kids are taken care of, we'll go straight home and get all that stuff out again."

Kate frowned. The woman was protesting too much. She hadn't even been asked about their winter clothing. She sounded almost panicked, and so defensive, as if Kate had accused her of a crime.

The man made no move to accept the clipboard. It was still in Kate's outstretched hand.

And then the oldest child, the pretty little girl, laughed harshly and muttered under her breath, "Yeah, right. Go straight home? How can we go straight home, Mama, when we don't *have* a home?"

Both parents paled, wincing as if they'd been struck.

Kate understood immediately. This family hadn't come to Med Center because someone was sick or physically injured. Or because someone had a fever, or the flu.

They had come into ER because they had no place else to go.

Because they were homeless.

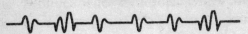

There was a low, steady hum of conversation in the ER waiting room, combined with the constant, droning voice of a television weathercaster. But in the corner Kate shared with the family, there was a long, painful moment of silence following the little girl's question, "How can we go straight home, Mama, when we don't *have* a home?"

Finally, the mother said softly, "Hush, Annie!" The father laughed self-consciously and said with what seemed to Kate to be a forced heartiness, "Now, honey, don't go telling fibs again, or you'll have this nice young lady thinking we're vagrants or something. You'll have her calling the police to put us out of this nice, warm hospital." His voice shook a little when he said the word "police."

The girl named Annie glared at both parents. But she said nothing.

The middle child, a boy of four or five, eased away from his father's side and, looking up into Kate's face with eyes far too serious for someone so young, said, "Annie's right, though. We don't got no home. Ours burned, in a big, big, fire." His eyes teared up, and he swiped at them angrily with dirty hands.

Shocked, Kate could only say, "I'm sorry. I'm really sorry."

The little boy leaned back against his father's chest again and instead of receiving a reprimand, got a sympathetic hug.

Kate turned her attention to the father. "Your house got caught in the refinery fire? You lived in Eastridge?" She lived there, too. It had been hit hardest by the fire.

He nodded. "We lived on the outskirts, down near the riverbank. It wasn't much, but it was all we had. We owned it, free and clear. Then the fire came. It took everything we had, plus, I got me some burns, bad ones on my back and shoulders, even my arms. I haven't been able to work since. We didn't have insurance. Couldn't afford the monthly payments."

"Everything we had," the woman echoed mournfully. "Gone."

This family needs help, Kate thought to herself. The problem was she didn't have a *clue* about where they should go to get it. She knew ER didn't have what they needed, but she didn't know what *would* help. It wasn't

33

hard to guess they had no money for a hotel room. And if they had friends or relatives to stay with, they wouldn't be here, would they? Did they even have money for meals?

"You're not going to tell, are you?" the mother asked anxiously, her voice still hushed. "We'll leave as soon as the weather lets up. You're not going to go get security and have them throw us out, are you?"

Kate was appalled. Throw them out into a freezing rainstorm? There were blizzard warnings already coming out over the television. High winds and huge amounts of snow were being predicted. How could she send three young children out into that? "No, no, of course not," she assured them quickly. "Let me get you some coffee. And some hot chocolate for the kids. I'll be right back." She saw the look on the father's face and hastily added, "It's free. It's right over there on that table by the door, see it? It's for anyone in the waiting room and," she added brightly, "you're in the waiting room, right?"

While she filled Styrofoam cups with coffee and hot chocolate, Kate's mind raced. She had to do something for these people. But what? In a way, the fact that the hospital was so busy was a good thing for the family. It was possible, given the fact that the weather was supposed to get much worse, that no one would notice the same five people sitting in the same spot all night long.

She was handling the charts right now. Maybe she could figure out a way to make it look like they were just waiting for a ride. She could always say their ride wasn't able to make it to the hospital before morning. Then they'd have the whole night to stay inside where it was nice and warm. In the meantime, maybe she could talk to someone in Social Services, to see what might be available for the family.

But she had to get back to ER, too. Her mother would be wondering what was taking her so long in the waiting room. At least three ambulances had arrived since Kate had walked into the waiting room. She'd be needed.

When she had handed the steaming cups carefully to the family members, she asked their names. "Jake and Ruth Sloan," the man answered. "And," waving a hand to include all three children, "these here are Annie, who's seven, and Paulie, who's five, and that little one there is Joanie."

"Listen," Kate said quickly, her voice low, "you can stay here tonight. It's busy, it's crowded, and it's probably going to get worse. No one will even notice that you've been here a while. If you can find enough chairs, why don't you stretch out and get some sleep? You can't go out in this awful storm." Almost as an afterthought, she added, "Have you had dinner?"

The man stiffened in his chair. "Sure, we have. I feed my family, miss, don't you worry about that."

Even if Kate hadn't guessed that he was lying, the look on Annie's face gave away the truth. Still, she let it drop. The man should be allowed to keep whatever pride he had left. But she would find a way to see that these children were fed.

"I'll come back in later and check on you," she told them. "Are you warm enough?"

"A lot warmer than we would be outside," the man said, allowing a small smile. Then he added quietly, "Thanks for being so nice, miss. We appreciate it."

"No problem. Relax, okay? No one's going to haul you out of here, not if I have anything to say about it. I'll be back later."

Paulie smiled at her, and waved as she left.

I may not have a lot, Kate thought as she went to find her mother. My house is small and Eastridge is certainly not the greatest neighborhood. I don't have a clue where I'm going to find the money for college and medical school, but at least I have a home, someplace I can go every day and every night. What is it like not to have even that much, through no fault of your own? To have no roof

36

over your head, no walls to keep out the rain and wind and snow? What would that be like?

"So," Abby asked Susannah when the Benz was crawling at a snail's pace along a now icy Linden Boulevard toward Med Center, "how was your date last night with that cute new intern?"

"Don't ask," Susannah answered darkly, peering through the windshield. The wipers scraped back and forth, doing their best. But the freezing rain was sticking to the glass. "I don't know why I ever told Alec Blackstone I would go out with him."

"Because Will Jackson pushed you to," Abby said matter-of-factly. "And that hurt your feelings. Will's supposed to be nuts about you the same way you're nuts about him."

Susannah ignored her, concentrating instead on keeping the car from skidding on the slick surface. Her headlights showed only the glassy boulevard stretching ahead of her. There were no other cars.

"Will hurt your pride," Abby continued blithely. "You were so mad that you decided to say yes to Alec, even though he doesn't ring your chimes. I tried to *tell* you, Will only pushed you into dating the guy because he wants to be absolutely sure you know what you're doing, getting involved with him. Will,

I mean. He's scared for you, Susannah. There are people out here in Grant who won't be exactly thrilled to see you with an African-American. The daughter of Samuel Grant II with Will Jackson? Some of those narrow-minded people could get nasty."

"I know. Sam already gave me that lecture, Abby. You don't need to repeat it."

"All I'm saying is, Will *is* nuts about you, and he doesn't want to see you get hassled. He pushed Alec off on you because he thought he'd be better for you. Safer. Alec *is* awfully cute, Susannah," she added with an impish grin. "And he's smart, and almost a doctor. Your parents would be thrilled. I heard his family has loads of cash. Country clubs, yachts, all that junk, just like you. Every nurse at Grant Memorial is panting after him."

An ambulance raced up behind them and, red light flashing, roared past them. Up ahead, Susannah saw another one speeding around the curve into Med Center's emergency entrance. How could they go so fast? Maybe the patients inside were so critical, the driver had no choice. In a critical case, minutes could make the difference. Still, it was risky, driving that fast.

A few feet up ahead, a car, its lights off, had spun out of control and sat with its front half parked on a lawn, the rear half extending a few feet out into the street, as if it hadn't been able to make up its mind whether or not to stay where it was. The driver didn't seem to be around. Gone in search of warm refuge, Susannah decided.

"That's Callie Matthews's car," Abby said. "It looks like she lost control. *That* must have made her mad. Callie doesn't like it when things *or* people don't do what she wants them to. So, anyway, tell me more about Alec."

"Well, he may be cute, and he may be smart and rich," Susannah said, steering carefully around the back end of the blue sports car, "but to tell you the truth, he's *boring*. Alec Blackstone's favorite topic of conversation is Alec Blackstone. And then he had the nerve to act hurt and insulted because I didn't throw myself into his arms at the end of the evening. You know what he actually *said* to me when he was leaving? 'I forgot you're just a high school kid. I guess I'd better stick to more mature women from now on.' "

Abby laughed. "Well, you *are* a high school kid."

"Yeah, but he made it sound like I'd never been kissed before. So I told him, flat out, that I only got kissed when I *wanted* to be kissed. He didn't like that very much."

"Well, good for you! Wait, Susannah! There's Callie."

Startled, Susannah forgot about the ice and slammed on the brake. The tires squealed a protest and the car began spinning wildly out of control. It slid in a circle, turning completely around in the middle of the street twice before Susannah regained control.

They hadn't hit anything. Not even Callie, who ran up to the car when it came to a stop and began pounding on Susannah's window.

Trembling, Susannah rolled the window down. "What are you *doing*, standing in the middle of the road like that?" she cried. "I almost hit you!"

"Let me in," Callie demanded. "I'm freezing!" Tiny drops of sleet coated her red jacket, wide-brimmed hat, and the blonde curls trailing out from underneath her collar. Her upturned nose was red with cold, thin black stripes of mascara ran from her eyelashes to her jaw, and her teeth were chattering.

"You'll have to get in Abby's side. Go around."

Callie slipped twice and almost fell as she scurried around the front of the car to push in beside Abby. "You should have taken the Jeep tonight, Susannah," she grumbled, shaking water drops from her coat and hat. "There isn't room in this stupid car for three people."

"Well, you could get back out," Abby

said, "and wait for someone else to pick you up. As you can see," she added sarcastically, "the boulevard is thriving with traffic, so it shouldn't be more than a few *hours* before you get another ride."

"Very funny, Abigail. I'm already frozen." Callie ripped her hat off and began fingering the long, blonde waves, pushing them into place. "I saw *six* ambulances while I was standing there in the freezing rain, and not *one* of them stopped to pick me up! I'm going to speak to my father about that." Her father, Caleb Matthews, was chief administrator of Med Center, a fact that his daughter shared with everyone she met. "I'll bet your Will Jackson was on one of those runs, Susannah," she added emphatically. "And he *knows* who I am."

Susannah set the car in motion again. She liked the sound of "your Will Jackson." Callie had twice caught her kissing Will, and amazingly, hadn't made a big deal out of it. Well, that wasn't exactly true. The second time, she'd gone running to Astrid Thompson, Kate's mother. Instead of speaking directly to Susannah, Astrid had gone to Sam to express her concern. And Sam had delivered that message to his twin sister. People in Grant might be upset if they saw Samuel Grant II's daughter walking down the street with an African-

American. Sam had meant well. Astrid had, too. But it had still been hard for Susannah to hear the truth.

As far as Susannah knew, Callie hadn't run up and down the streets of Grant shouting out the latest gossip. For that, Susannah was grateful. "Callie, has it crossed your mind that the people in those ambulances might be so critically injured or ill that even taking a few minutes to stop and pick you up could mean the difference between life and death? The paramedics aren't allowed to take on passengers. What were you doing out in the first place?"

"I was going to get my father. With the weather the way it is, he won't come home tonight if I don't yank him away from Emsee now. If the power goes out, like they're saying it might, I don't want to be home with just my mother in a dark, cold house." Callie's mother was a semi-invalid, a victim of chronic kidney disease. Except for her visits to Med Center for dialysis treatments, she seldom left the house.

"Why didn't you just call him and ask him to come home?" Abby, squeezed in between Susannah and Callie, asked.

Callie was still shivering with cold. "All I ever get when I call is his machine. My chances of dragging him out of there are better in person."

Susannah, turning the car into Med Center's wide, tree-lined driveway, didn't think those chances were very good. She didn't much like Callie's father. He was overbearing and pompous, but she had to admit he *was* dedicated to the medical complex. If the weather didn't improve, he wouldn't want to leave the hospital, not even for his wife and daughter. He'd know how hectic things were likely to get, and he'd want to be there to make sure things went as smoothly as possible.

Susannah parked in the parking garage, and the three of them made a mad dash for the entrance to emergency.

chapter
5

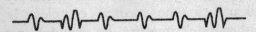

Because of the chorus of ambulance sirens they'd heard on the way over, Susannah wasn't surprised to find the ER hallways crowded with gurneys and the waiting room filled to overflowing.

"This is only the beginning," she said in the lounge when Callie had gone upstairs to her father's office without so much as a thank-you. Abby had made a quick call to her house, then joined Susannah in the lounge. Susannah slipped out of her coat to don her pink smock and smooth her hair. "Things could get a lot worse before the night's over."

"I don't think I'm going to like this," Abby said glumly. "There's going to be a lot of blood, *isn't* there?"

"Only in the treatment and trauma rooms. Relax, you're not allowed in there." Susannah straightened her collar and glanced around for some sign of Will. She didn't see him. "Kate's mom will keep you busy out here, probably toting med supplies from one room to another. You won't mind that, will you? Or maybe she'll send you to the waiting room to help with charts or with relatives. That's right up your alley, Abby. You're so good with people."

"Flattery will get you nowhere. I don't know why I let you talk me into this."

Susannah laughed. "I *didn't*. You were willing. You wanted something to do while Sid was on his home visit. Now, when he gets back, he'll know exactly where to look for you."

"*If* he gets back here." Abby checked her round, rosy face in the mirror, and pushed her thick, dark waves into place. "Maybe he won't make it back tonight." There was anxiety in her voice as she added, "I wish the weather had been better for his first time driving. I mean, *we* almost didn't get here, right?"

"Yeah, but you *did* get here," Kate said, as she came into the room. "Hi, guys. Boy, am I glad to see you! It's been wild. Thanks for filling in, O'Connor. We can't afford to be short-handed tonight. Where's Mom putting you?"

Abby shrugged. "I don't know yet. It doesn't matter, as long as she keeps me away from the sight and smell of anything red and sticky."

Kate laughed. "I thought you were planning

to go into the medical field. And you can't stand the sight of blood?"

"Me? No way," Abby said firmly. "I'm going to be a social worker."

That seemed to surprise Kate. "You are? Well, then, listen, you might know what to do about this family I met in the — "

She was interrupted by the arrival of two nurses, complaining about the weather, and her mother. The head nurse seemed delighted to see the new arrivals. She dispatched Susannah immediately to trauma room C to help with the suturing of a severe laceration suffered in a car wreck, asked Abby to go upstairs to linen supply and bring down a fresh batch of disposable sheets, and sent Kate to treatment room three where a toddler was being treated for a croup attack. "You can hold his hand and talk to him while he's under the croup tent," Kate's mother said as she left the room.

When she had gone, Kate turned to Abby. "I need to talk to you. When we all have a minute free, okay?"

Then they all departed, anxious to begin helping.

Thirty minutes later, Susannah was on her way to the nurses' station when she saw Will, in his navy blue paramedic's jacket, his dark, curly head bare. His back was to her, but she'd know that loose, casual, confident walk anywhere.

Without thinking, she called his name. Then she remembered she was mad at him for pushing her into a date with that bore, Alec Blackstone.

Too late. Will had already turned around. He was waiting, smiling at her.

She refused to admit to Will Jackson that last night's date hadn't been exactly the most stimulating experience of her life. "Give it a try," he had urged when he'd learned from Kate that Alec was interested in Susannah. "He seems like an okay guy. Your folks would like him."

Susannah had been furious. How could Will push her into the arms of some other guy?

"He ask you out yet?" Will had asked her after seeing Alec talking to Susannah in the corridor. Will's face was tight and closed against her. She knew that look so well. "You should go," he went on before she could answer. "He seems like a nice enough guy. And I hear he comes from big bucks."

She knew what he was inferring. *She* had money, and Alec Blackstone had money, therefore they belonged together. Two of a kind.

Not. What a ridiculous idea! What was the *matter* with him? Did he really think she was that shallow?

She'd been hurt by Will's suggestion. She was *still* hurt, and if he asked her how her date was, she'd stomp down on his foot. He deserved it.

"Hey," he said to Susannah as she approached him, "how about this weather? We've been on so many runs, the unit's beginning to feel like my second home. And it's a major challenge just getting from one accident site to the other. We've been sliding all over the place. No serious injuries so far, though. I guess people are scared by the ice, and are taking it easy out there. Did you have any trouble getting here?"

Susannah wondered if he was deliberately avoiding the question of her date, or if he really wasn't even thinking about it. Maybe he just didn't care. Or did he?

Then the words broke free. "I had a great time last night," she said, with defiance, daring him to contradict her. And suddenly she recognized the look on his face: pain. Well, he had it coming.

"Oh, yeah?" His voice, deliberately casual, stung Susannah.

So she twisted the knife a little. As they began walking, weaving their way among the gurneys and medical carts and staff members hurrying along, she said, "We went to Antoine's, you know, that French restaurant in the Grisham Hotel downtown?"

Will shook his head. "Haven't been to a French restaurant in, oh, say, a lifetime. Fast food, burgers — that's more my speed. But," he added hastily, "I'm glad you had fun." In that same, maddeningly casual tone of voice, he said, "Going to do it again, I guess? I mean, since you had such a good time."

It was as if there were two of Susannah then. One who wanted desperately to blurt out, "No, Will, I'm not going to do it again because I can't stand the guy and I'd rather be with you," and a second Susannah who wanted to declare, "Yes, yes, I'm going to go out with him again and again and again, because he's rich and my parents will like him and we'll get married and live in a mansion just like Linden Hall. And I *won't* work in your clinic in Eastridge. After all, if I would marry someone so self-centered and spoiled, I obviously don't care about people the way you do. And isn't that what you really think of me, Will Jackson?"

She said neither. All she could manage was, "I don't know if I'll be going out with him again."

And then, there he was. Alec Blackstone.

He was looking crisp and handsome and arrogant, and smiling at Susannah as if to say, "Look, you lucky girl, here I am again!" and barely acknowledging Will with a dismissive nod.

"Well, *hi*, there," Alec said, reaching out to take one of Susannah's hands in his, his straight, even, white teeth practically blinding her, "isn't this weather wild? I expect to get plenty of practice tonight. I couldn't have asked for better weather."

"Now *there's* an attitude," Will muttered, and the hostility in his voice warmed Susannah's heart. It sounded like jealousy to *her*. "This place is busting at the seams with cuts and bruises and broken bones and some very scared patients, and to this guy, it's an opportunity."

Barely restraining a wicked grin, Susannah turned away from Alec to whisper in an aside to Will, "You were the one who said he was a nice guy."

"So I was wrong." Having said that, Will turned and strode away, his head high, his shoulders back, his spine as stiff and rigid as a flagpole. His usual, casual saunter was completely absent.

Susannah wanted to laugh aloud. If that wasn't jealousy, she'd eat her smock.

"So," Alec said, the confident smile still on his handsome face, "when you get a break, you want to go downstairs for coffee?"

She returned his smile with one of her own. "I don't *think* so, Alec. I'm not *mature* enough to drink coffee." The smile still on her face, she turned and hurried over to Astrid to find out where she was needed next.

There were auto accident victims in trauma room D, a fisherwoman who'd fallen through the ice on the river in treatment room six, and in treatment room four, an elderly man who had had a heart attack after falling on an icy sidewalk.

Susannah took a warming blanket to the ice fisherwoman, then went into the crowded waiting room to bring the wife of the cardiac case a cup of hot coffee and talk to her soothingly. She didn't mention that when she'd left the man's room, Dr. Lincoln had already delivered three hundred volts of electricity to the patient's chest. The result had been a dismal flatline on the monitor. The man probably wasn't going to make it. But that wasn't information volunteers were supposed to share with relatives.

Someday, when she was a full-fledged doctor, she *would* have to deliver that kind of news. Susannah wasn't looking forward to it.

But it was part of the profession. No one had to tell her that. Death happened, even in as fine a facility as Med Center. Still, in the months since she'd begun volunteering, they'd saved a whole lot more lives than they'd lost. Focusing on that made her feel better.

~~~~~~~~~~~~~~~~~~~~~~

Susannah was on her way to get more supplies when she thought she caught a glimpse of her brother's fair hair. It couldn't be Sam, she told herself. Not on a Friday night. He'd be out partying with his friends. Wasn't he the very person who had said repeatedly that he couldn't understand what she saw in Med Center, why she spent so much time here?

But it *was* Sam, Susannah realized as she drew closer. She also realized *why* he was there. Sam had his eye on Lily Dolan, a nurse's aide who, as far as Susannah knew, wasn't on duty tonight. But Sam probably didn't know that. Lily hadn't taken much interest in Sam, so it wasn't surprising that he didn't know her schedule. She wouldn't have shared that with him.

Although Lily Dolan was the same age as the twins, she had graduated from Grant High a year earlier, at sixteen. Because her parents had little money, she had taken the job at Med Center to save for college. She was a tall, beautiful girl with long, wildly curly, auburn hair and deep blue eyes that alternately registered cynicism, suspicion, and sly humor.

Lily seemed much too old and wise for someone only seventeen. Susannah had never once seen her leaning leisurely against a wall or sitting on the worn tweed couch in the lounge or parked in a chair reading a magazine during a rare lull in emergency traffic. If there was nothing pressing to do, Lily *created* something to do.

"That girl doesn't know how to relax," Astrid had said once, immediately after she'd scolded Lily for failing to restrain the auburn curls that fell to her shoulders. Lily had hastily apologized, and rushed off again, wrestling with the undisciplined strands as she ran.

Although Lily was stunning, with smooth, fair, perfect skin and that incredible hair, Susannah had never seen her out and about in Grant with a boy at her side, nor did any boy ever come to emergency's back entrance to wait for Lily following her shift.

"If you ask me, Sam's wasting his time," Abby had said one night recently when she'd come from Rehab to ride home with Susannah. She had spotted Sam, sitting in the waiting room, reading, and guessed why he was there. "Lily Dolan didn't date all through high school, so why would she start now? I mean, your brother's gorgeous and rich, but so are lots of other guys in Grant, and Lily has never given them the time of day. She didn't even go to her own senior prom. Not that she didn't have plenty of offers."

Everyone in the hospital knew that Lily's father, Tommy Dolan, was a drunk. He'd been admitted to the ER more than once. Sometimes it was because he'd been stupid enough to get behind the wheel of a car, which in the past had brought him face-to-face with a tree, a brick wall, and other cars. Other times, he was brought in because he'd been fighting in a local bar. Dolan had a terrible temper. The police were kind enough to take him to the ER to have his bloodied knuckles and black eyes treated before they carted him off to jail.

It was hard to believe that Lily, who was so gentle, so tender, could be related to someone so violent.

After hearing the stories about Lily's father, Susannah understood why Lily didn't date. Maybe she thought all men were like him. And while that wasn't really fair of Lily, who could blame her?

But Lily had a temper, too. Susannah had seen it once in the cafeteria when a nurse accidentally spilled hot coffee down Lily's shoulders and back. Lily had jumped from her chair, screaming in pain, and had whirled on the embarrassed nurse in fury. Her reaction astonished everyone within hearing distance.

Then, Lily had realized what was happening. She stopped in midshout. Her beautiful face, scarlet with rage, drained instantly of every last ounce of color, and she gasped in horror and shame. "Oh, God, I'm sorry, I'm sorry!" she cried, and turned and ran from the cafeteria, leaving behind her a shocked, pained silence.

"Got her father's temper, that girl," an orderly sitting behind Susannah had muttered. "She'd better watch it or it'll get her in trouble, just like it has him."

Susannah, remembering the horror in Lily's eyes, thought that was probably exactly what Lily was afraid of. She hadn't seen her lose her temper since that day.

"Where is she?" Sam demanded when Susannah reached him.

"I haven't seen her. She's not on duty tonight, I guess. Didn't she tell you that?"

Sam's handsome face looked glum. "She never tells me anything. She barely says hello. She looks right through me. It's like I'm invisible."

"Oh, Sam. It's not your fault. Lily doesn't trust guys, that's all. I guess she thinks they're all like her father."

The glumness turned to revulsion. "I'm not *anything* like Tommy Dolan!"

"I know that." Sam liked women, and except for the fact that his affections were no more lasting than a late April snow, he treated them with respect. "But Lily doesn't."

"Well, how's she going to find out if she won't go out with me?"

Susannah had to laugh. "Sam, if you could see yourself. You look like a little four-year-old who's just been told the other kids don't want to play with him." It was so like Sam to go after one of the few girls in town who expressed no interest in him. "Anyway," she added briskly, aware that the pace in the corridors had stepped up again, "what's the weather like out there? Any better than it was an hour ago?"

"Are you kidding? It's worse! There's ice on everything. And now the sleet is turning to snow. Linden Boulevard is going to look like a wrecking yard. So," Sam added anxiously, "Lily's not coming in?"

Susannah heard an approaching siren. It died just beyond the entrance. Calling over her shoulder, "I don't know. Ask Astrid!" She ran to meet the ambulance.

Will was one of the paramedics. When he came running in pushing the gurney, he mouthed the word, "Burns," and Susannah's heart sank. How she hated to see burn patients! Even the less serious cases suffered intensely. The more serious ones, like the patients they'd had during the refinery fire, were transferred after initial treatment in ER to the Burn Center on the grounds, so it wasn't always easy to find out how they were doing. This new patient was a little boy, only four, who had accidentally overturned a space heater in his grandparents' home while they thought he was safely asleep upstairs.

When Kate joined Will and Susannah in the trauma room, she asked Will if Damon had been at the fire. Will nodded. "Yeah. He's fine. The fire's out. It was just the boy's bedroom. I don't know how that fire truck got there so fast with the roads the way they are, but it did." He laughed shortly. "Maybe Damon was driving. And my guess is, he was the first one out of the truck."

Kate nodded in agreement. "Absolutely. Isn't he always?"

The little boy's clothing was cut off and Susannah handed one of the nurses gauze pads to apply to the burns. Another nurse held aloft a bottle of sterile saline solution to pour over the gauze. Dr. Jonah Izbecki, Susannah's favorite physician in ER, listened to his breathing. A third nurse called out vital statistics, while a young resident Susannah knew only as Tim continued to give the patient oxygen. Chest X rays were ordered, and blood tests, and Kate was assigned to deliver the blood to the lab. She did it quickly and efficiently, hurrying through the hall purposefully.

"He's so little," Kate murmured to Will when she returned to the room. "Was he breathing when you brought him in?"

"Breathing *and* talking. Something about Juniper. His grandmother told us he meant his teddy bear. They couldn't find it. I guess poor old Juniper wasn't as lucky as the kid."

Kate turned and left the room again. She was back almost immediately, a fat, yellow, stuffed toy in her hands. "It's not Juniper, but maybe he'll settle for Winnie the Pooh. I borrowed this one from the pediatric waiting room." She went over to the table and, holding the toy aloft, glanced inquiringly at Dr. Izbecki.

He shook his head no. His hands continued to move across the boy's chest as he spoke. "Not now. You'll contaminate the area. But," he added quietly, "save it for later."

Holding the stuffed bear, Kate returned to Will. She asked if he thought the little boy was in any pain.

"Not yet."

But they both knew he would be.

"How bad, do you think?" Kate wanted to know. Will had seen many more burn cases than she had, and could gauge the extent of the burns.

"I can't tell. It's not as bad as it could have been. We figure, no more than ten percent third degree, the rest second degree. Mostly his back and legs, looked like."

Kate was relieved. Still, second-degree burns would mean a lot of pain as he recovered. And then there was the smoke damage, always the most dangerous side effect of any fire. Had Damon and his team pulled this child out in time?

"Lungs don't sound too bad," Izbecki announced, and there was a small sigh of relief around the table. "Keep that oxygen going! Finish the pads, and then get him over to the Burn Center, stat!"

While she was relieved that the damage hadn't been worse, Kate was sorry to see the boy leave. Kate glanced at the boy's chart. His name was Robert King. She'd have to remember that so she could call the Burn Center later and see how he was doing.

At the last minute, she reached out impulsively and propped Winnie the Pooh up beside the bandaged right arm. It would be there when Robert awoke. She hoped he would sleep for a very long time, keeping the pain at bay as long as possible.

When they left the trauma room, there was no time for Susannah, Kate, and Will to talk about the case. Will was immediately called out on a run to an auto accident. Kate returned to the waiting room to check on the family she'd talked to earlier, and Susannah was called into a treatment room where Dr. Lincoln was neatly stitching a deep laceration in the palm of an elderly woman's hand.

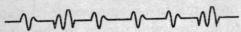

Sid Costello, struggling to keep the Med Center rehab van on the slick highway, was wishing he'd listened to his mother.

"Stay here tonight," she had urged as he shrugged into his blue-and-white Grant football jacket. "You can't go out in this. The roads are terrible, and getting worse all the time."

"I'm supposed to be back at Rehab by ten." It sounded silly, even to him. All he had to do was make a call, and he'd be given permission to stay overnight at his mother's house. No one would expect him back tonight, not in this weather. But he hadn't seen Abby since Wednesday. That was way too long, even on good days, and today hadn't been an especially good day. It was really hard seeing the look in his mother's and grandfather's eyes as he wheeled his chair through the house. He was used to that chair . . . almost. They weren't.

Sid knew that during all of these months in rehab his mother had never given up hope that he'd walk again. He hadn't, either, but the truth was, it hadn't happened yet. So he needed the chair, unless he wanted to lie in bed all day. This was his first visit home, and he could see that the sight of him navigating on wheels instead of legs had stunned his family. It was as if, for the first time, his mother understood that the chair might be a part of her son's life forever. She wasn't handling that very well.

Abby *did* handle it well, though. And he needed to see her. He needed to see her smiling face and the glint in her dark eyes when she said, "Hey, Costello, just because you're in that chair doesn't mean you can take it easy. Get over here and help me fold these towels."

Abby made him feel whole.

But he'd made a mistake, Sid realized angrily as the van skidded dizzily into the curb on the driver's side. He had practiced on the van many times, but only on the grounds of Med Center, and only in good weather. Sun shining, sky clear, roads dry. That was a far cry from what he was driving in now. *Trying* to drive in. It was hopeless. Joey Rudd, the orderly who had taught him how to use the hand controls posted near the steering wheel, had said, "All you gotta do is steer, practically."

But how could he steer when he couldn't *see*? The snow was coming down thick and fast now, and as if that weren't bad enough, the wicked wind was creating giant drifts in his path. He'd already hit two that were so deep, he'd been forced to steer around them.

Only the thought of Abby, waiting for him in ER, kept him hunched over the steering wheel, peering intently through the white-coated windshield into the dark, deserted night, feeding gas to the van's engine. His back and shoulders ached, and he felt like he'd been driving for hours. How much further could it be to Med Center?

If only he could see . . .

When Kate reached the waiting room, it was still full, packed with anxious relatives. The Sloan family hadn't left. The two younger children were asleep, the baby in its mother's arms, the little boy slumped with his back against the arms of a blue plastic chair, his feet lying in his father's lap. Mr. Sloan had removed his own jacket to place over the boy's legs. Annie, her expression sullen, stood against the wall, her bare, spindly legs in sagging white socks and sneakers crossed, her arms folded over her chest.

She should have jeans on, Kate thought, not a cotton dress.

The father lifted his head, smiling in recognition as Kate approached. She wanted to get them all something to eat, but she knew it was important to do it without putting a serious dent in the man's pride. With that in mind, she had taken a quick detour to the basement kitchen to speak to the head cook.

Might as well dive right in, she finally decided when she had said hello, getting in return only a cold glare from Annie. "Listen, I wish you guys hadn't eaten," Kate said, taking a seat beside the mother. "So many of the patients don't eat their meals." She laughed lightly. "I guess there's nothing like major surgery to clobber a healthy appetite. I think it's a crime to waste so much food. They just throw it out, you know. The law says they have to. If you were hungry, you could really help them out downstairs in the kitchen."

Kate saw the look on Mr. Sloan's face. The man wasn't stupid. She read refusal in his eyes. But just then, Paulie awakened, rubbed his eyes sleepily, and said plaintively, "I'm awful hungry, Daddy."

Without a word, Mr. Sloan gently moved his son's feet aside. He stood, picked up the little boy, and walked over to take Annie's hand. He motioned to his wife to join them. All he said to Kate was, "Where do we go?"

Kate was impressed by the man's quiet dignity. He didn't want to take from others, but his children were hungry. His pride had to come second to that.

Relieved, Kate led the way downstairs to the kitchen. Five trays of covered metal and plastic dishes were already waiting on a small table in an alcove just outside the double kitchen doors. The alcove was occupied only by a tall, three-tier, metal food rack and a broom. The family could eat in peace, leave when they were finished, and not a soul would see or speak to them. The cook had promised Kate.

She didn't insult them by thanking them for "helping out." Even Annie would see through that, and she'd be humiliated. "Enjoy!" was all Kate said as she turned to leave. "See you upstairs!"

A young voice called after her, "I don't *like* meat loaf!"

Kate grinned as she stepped into the elevator. Atta girl, Annie, she thought with admiration. Don't pretend to like something just because it's free. No matter how tough things get. But she hoped that Annie would eat the meal.

Upstairs in ER, Susannah was leaving a trauma room, her arms filled with disposable linens headed for the trash bin when Lily Dolan, her wiry, red hair sparkling with melting snowflakes, her fair skin rosy with cold, rushed in through the back door. As she ran, she ripped off her long, black raincoat and gloves, revealing her pale blue nurse's aide's pantsuit. Spotting Susannah, she said breath-lessly, "Astrid called me. Two other aides live out in the boondocks and couldn't make it in. I had to take the bus, that's why it took me so long. My dad wouldn't let me take the car. He said he needed it." Lily laughed scornfully, and darted into the lounge to grab a quick cup of coffee. When Susannah joined her, she added in that same contemptuous tone of voice, "I guess he wanted to make sure he could get to a bar in case the ones in our neighborhood are closed."

Susannah was surprised. Lily seldom took the time to talk to anyone at the hospital. Any time she *had* spoken briefly with Susannah, she had never once mentioned her family.

It wasn't until Lily turned to put sugar in her coffee that Susannah saw the ugly red mark on one cheek. It was swollen, and begin-ning to turn from red to purple.

She was horrified. No one had to tell her who was responsible. The argument over who was going to take the family car must have been a bad one.

Why did Lily, and probably her mother, too, take the abuse? Why didn't they just leave?

Maybe they don't have anyplace else to go, Susannah thought to herself.

Absentmindedly rubbing the inflamed cheekbone, Lily asked, "Has it been horrendous here? Astrid said on the phone that you'd been really busy because of the weather. Has the pace eased up at all?"

A dying siren outside, immediately followed by another, interrupted Susannah's answer.

Lily laughed ruefully. "Well, I guess that answers my question. Come on, let's get to work!"

Susannah, unable to come up with a tactful way to phrase a question about the glaring red streak on Lily's cheek, nodded and led the way out of the room. But she had made up her mind that somehow, she would think of a way to talk to Lily about what was going on at her house.

"What happened to Lily's face?" Abby asked in a low voice as she joined them in their rush to the back door.

"Guess," Susannah answered grimly.

Abby nodded, her lips tightening. "Somebody should do something about him," she said.

Then they were standing under the outside canopy in thick, wind-whipped snow, shivering as they awaited the gurneys being lifted from the vehicles.

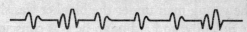
Susannah was surprised to see Sam vigorously shoveling snow off the driveway and tossing it aside. It was immediately blown back into his face, but he persevered. He looked almost happy, his cheeks red, his eyes bright.

Sam glanced up and, spotting Lily, dropped the shovel and advanced toward the group clustered under the canopy. But he was too late. The first gurney was already out of the ambulance and Lily was one of the first to grasp its sides and begin pushing. Her back was already disappearing. Disappointed, Sam returned to his shovel.

The patients from the first ambulance were members of a hiking party. They had taken to the hills early that morning, before the rain began and the temperature plummeted. The first two hikers, although suffering from exposure, had only minor injuries. But the third had taken a bad fall, landing on his stomach on a sharp-edged boulder.

"Some tenderness and ecchymosis in the

right upper abdomen," Will told the doctors, "pulse one-ten, respirations twenty, blood pressure, one twenty-six over eighty. He's mildly hypothermic. We warmed the IV solution before we started it."

The young man under the blanket was shivering violently, and although he was conscious, he didn't seem to know where he was. Susannah knew the "ecchymosis" Will had mentioned referred to severe bruising and could indicate internal injuries, which might be life-threatening.

The patient's lack of control in his hands, arms and legs shook the gurney as they ran with it. He appeared to Susannah to be completely exhausted, and when he spoke, asking about his friends, his speech was slow and slurred, as if he'd been drinking. The slurring was a common sign of hypothermia. Susannah had seen several cases like his when an explosion in the chem lab had pinned victims under rubble in freezing temperatures. When they were finally extricated, many of them had these same symptoms.

She was glad Will had had the experience and know-how to warm the IV solution before administering it to this particular patient. Cold fluids would almost certainly have been harmful.

In the treatment room, the patient was

placed under a warming blanket and immediately hooked up to a cardiac monitor. His rapidly sinking blood pressure combined with Dr. Izbecki's gentle palpation of the bruised abdomen verified internal injuries. The young man was taken upstairs to surgery less than five minutes after his arrival in ER.

In the meantime, the patients from the second ambulance, victims of a serious car accident, had arrived in ER. One, a sixteen-year-old girl Abby knew, had suffered a serious chest injury. She was restless, frightened, and confused.

Abby tried her best to calm the girl so blood pressure and blood tests could be taken, but the girl, whose name was Amanda, kept waving her arms about wildly and shouting.

"Portable X ray," Dr. Lincoln ordered when the gurney was in place. "We need chest, and lateral cervical spine. Arterial blood gases, stat, and get someone down here from cardiopulmonary. Barlow, if he's available. I think we're going to need him."

Almost immediately, the monitor revealed a tachycardia, which told Susannah that the girl's heart was beating too fast. One possibility, she knew from similar cases, was that the chest injury had caused bleeding, and the heart was being squeezed by the blood collecting in the sac around the organ. That would explain the paleness of the girl's skin showing beneath the oxygen mask.

If that was the case, a needle would have to be inserted beneath her ribs to draw off the blood. It was a painful procedure, and Susannah knew Dr. Lincoln disliked doing it. She must suspect the condition, called cardiac tamponade, or she wouldn't have called for Jeremy Barlow's father, Thomas Barlow, head of cardiopulmonary.

The tall, distinguished doctor arrived moments later, and he was not at *all* happy when he saw the condition of the girl lying on the table. Glancing at her chart, he barked, "Her blood pressure's in the basement. Why wasn't she sent immediately to surgery? We're wasting valuable time here."

Ignoring Dr. Lincoln completely, he signaled to two orderlies standing by to grab the gurney and wheel it to the elevator. When they had done so, he strode out of the room without another word, just as he'd arrived.

"Whew!" Dr. Lincoln brushed a lock of dark, wavy hair away from her face with one plastic-gloved hand. She gazed after the departing doctor in awe. "That man really fills up a room, doesn't he?"

Susannah exchanged a glance with Abby. They had both said the same thing about Jeremy's father, more than once.

"He doesn't seem like the kind of man a woman would leave," the doctor mused aloud. She was referring to Bianca Barlow, Jeremy's mother, who had left the family home the year before to pursue a writing career in San Francisco. "But then, who knows what goes on in someone's home?"

Susannah remembered the cruel mark on Lily Dolan's cheek, and nodded in agreement.

The remaining accident victims had been luckier than Amanda. A broken arm was set, facial lacerations were stitched, and the driver of the car was treated for concussion and kept overnight for observation.

When a brief, luxurious moment of quiet fell over the ER, Abby, Kate, and Susannah retreated to the lounge for a welcome break.

Callie Matthews had no luck persuading her father to leave his enormous mahogany desk and come home with her.

"Tell you what," Caleb Matthews said. "Why don't you run downstairs and get us something to eat? We'll eat it here, just the two of us." He smiled benevolently, but Callie knew it was only because he hated to see her pout. "Even on a night like this, I guess I can spare twenty minutes or so for my girl. We'll have a picnic, right here in my office."

"Can't we at least go to the cafeteria?" Callie

loved walking into the busy hospital cafeteria in the company of its administrator. And maybe Sam would be there. Any chance to spend time with Sam should not be overlooked. As long as there was any chance at all that one day, Sam would quit thinking of Callie Matthews as just a casual date and realize that they belonged together, she wasn't giving up. She spent a lot of time thinking about what gorgeous children she and Sam would have. If he didn't shape up pretty soon, she was going to make a serious play for that cute new intern. Maybe if Sam saw her out with another rich, gorgeous guy like himself, he'd realize he wasn't the only prize in the game. Maybe it would shake him up and he'd come looking for her. Finally!

Her father shook his head. "No cafeteria. It takes too long. I'll just call down to the kitchen and tell Eddie to fix us a couple of trays. He'll do it for me. Give us the best, take my word for it." He picked up the phone on his desk. "You be a good girl and run down and get it, okay? It'll save time. If we have to wait for the kitchen help to do it, we won't get it until midnight. And like I said, honey, I don't have a lot of time. We'll have to make this short and sweet."

Disgruntled, but telling herself that twenty

minutes was better than nothing, Callie stomped from the room.

In the basement, the elevator doors opened directly onto the small alcove where the Sloan family was just finishing up the hot, satisfying meal that Kate had arranged for them.

Callie stopped short just outside the elevator doors. Mouth agape, hands on her hips, she stared for several seconds before calling out sharply, "What on earth do you people think you're *doing*?"

chapter
9

Sid plowed on through the thick curtain of white, determined to reach the safety of Med Center, and Abby. He repeatedly hit icy spots in the road that sent his wheels spinning crazily and his heart plummeting into his stomach.

He was scared. There didn't seem to be anyone else out in this blinding sea of white. He'd seen a dozen cars or more stranded by the side of the road. Some were in ditches, some carefully parked when the driver had given up and abandoned the vehicle. He hadn't even seen a police car or an ambulance. Where the hell *was* everyone?

No one else is stupid enough to be out in this, he told himself in disgust.

Even as he continued to wrestle with the controls, fighting to keep the van on the road, he was agonizingly aware that if *he* got stranded like the drivers in those other cars, there wouldn't be a hell of a lot he could do about it. He couldn't very well jump down from the driver's seat, the way they had, and stalk off angrily to find shelter. Stalking off required the full use of one's legs.

And it wouldn't do him any good to unload himself and his chair from a stranded vehicle. The chair was great, but it didn't operate in deep snow.

Do *not*, Sid told himself through teeth that were clenched with anxiety, do *not* get this van stuck in a snowdrift. Keep it on the road and keep it going.

He tried. He tried with everything in him, thinking, Abby, I'm on my way, I'll be there any minute now. Med Center's got to be around here somewhere.

Another very long ten minutes passed before he realized with sickening certainty that he had taken a wrong turn somewhere. He was no longer on Massachusetts Avenue with its lighted shop windows and abundance of streetlights. He was instead on a dark, narrow, unfamiliar road flanked on both sides by thick woods.

Sid was stunned. How had this happened? Where had he made his mistake?

He was still trying to figure out how he'd gone astray when the van hit a slick patch of bare ice and began to slide crazily sideways.

Though he fought with all his might, Sid lost the battle. The van was bigger than he by far, and wildly out of control. It spun around twice before it sideswiped the thick, black trunk of a tree and skidded down an embankment, then finally came to rest in a deep snow ditch.

The van was white. Ghostlike, it sat tilted slightly in the ditch, hidden behind a curtain of snow.

There was no one else on the road. If someone did drive by, they would see nothing out of the ordinary. Snow was rapidly erasing the skid marks the van had made, and except for a slight mark on the bark of a tree trunk, there was no evidence that any vehicle had left the road and was at that moment stranded in the ditch below the embankment.

No evidence at all.

"I'm worried about Sid," Abby said nervously when she and Kate and Susannah were settled in the lounge, coffee in hand. "He should have called by now. Even if he decided to stay at his mother's house, which I hope he had the sense to do, he should have called from there to tell me."

Kate shrugged. "So, call his mom's house."

"I tried. I couldn't get through. Maybe some of the lines are down. Ours are still working, but I don't know who else to call. Sid was only going to his mom's house, and then coming back here. No one else is going to know where he might be. Or if he's okay."

"He'll be fine," Susannah said with conviction she wasn't sure she felt. Who could really be okay out there in that mess? And she knew this was Sid's first trip in the van. He'd driven it around the Emsee complex, but that wasn't the same as driving around the city, even in good weather. "You're always telling him he can take care of himself. That's how you got him to work harder in Rehab, remember? By telling him he could do anything."

Frowning, Abby nodded. "And he can. Usually. But this . . . this is different. I've never seen a snowstorm like this one."

"Blizzard," Lily Dolan pointed out as she walked into the room. The mark on her face was beginning to purple. "This is not a snowstorm, this is a blizzard. There's a difference." She poured a cup of coffee and turned to face the trio. "People *die* in blizzards."

Abby made a small sound of distress.

Susannah sent Lily a warning glance. To Abby, she said, "Sid probably stayed at his mom's, Abby. He wouldn't go out in this."

She received a skeptical glance from her best friend. "Are you kidding? You know Sid better than that. He planned to come back here.

That's what he planned to do. When Sid intends to do something, he doesn't let anybody or anything get in his way. Not even a blizzard."

The phone on the wall shrilled. Abby's face brightened. "Maybe that's him now," she cried, and ran to snatch up the receiver. Her face fell, and she extended the phone to Kate. "It's for you."

"For me?" Kate held the phone to her ear.

"You'd better get down here." She recognized the voice. It belonged to Eddie, the kitchen's head cook, the man who had been so helpful when she went to him about the homeless family. A huge, ruddy-faced man, he had a heart the size of Texas. "That Matthews kid is down here, and she's giving your people a hard time."

"Callie?" Kate groaned aloud. What was Callie *doing* in the basement? Damn it! "I'm on my way."

She hurried from the room, nearly colliding with Damon and Will, who were pushing a gurney. This was the cardiac case Will had phoned in a few minutes earlier. The man had been shoveling snow in spite of two previous heart attacks. On the gurney, a paramedic straddled the patient's chest, performing CPR, while Will continued to administer oxygen.

Damon, his black fireman's hat off, grabbed a crash cart that was sitting in the hallway and pushed it alongside.

Kate hesitated. She might be needed up here. Will had said the patient was in full arrest, which meant he wasn't breathing at all. They'd have to fight hard to save him.

But Susannah, Abby, and Lily were here, and it seemed to Kate that plenty of doctors and nurses were rushing toward the trauma room where Will was heading with the patient.

The family downstairs had no one but her.

Making up her mind, she scribbled her name on the sign-out sheet and ran for the stairs.

The scene she encountered at the foot of the stairs was sickening. Standing behind the small, cluttered table as if it were a shield, the Sloan family faced an indignant Callie. Eddie, in a massive white apron, was holding one of the metal double doors open, watching. There was a look of disgust on his face, flushed from the kitchen heat. The baby in Mrs. Sloan's arms was screaming, her arms waving wildly. Mr. Sloan, his own face white with shame, held Paulie by the hand. Annie stood with her back pressed against the metal food cart behind her, a trapped-rabbit look in her eyes.

"Callie!" Kate shouted as she burst out of the stairwell. "What are you doing down here?"

Callie whirled. She waved a hand to include the table, its scattered, empty dishes and mugs, and the family. "Shouldn't you be asking *them* that? Who *are* these people, anyway? They're obviously not kitchen help. So why are they eating our food?"

Kate laughed rudely. Kitchen help? Did people still call employees "kitchen help"? And what did she mean by "*our* food"? As if she owned the hospital. Her father didn't even own it. He just *ran* it, and he *didn't* pay for food out of his own pocket.

"These *people* are my friends," Kate said, her voice cool. "I invited them to eat here. If you have a problem with that, take it up with me, not them." To Mr. Sloan, she said, forcing false cheerfulness into her voice, "Why don't you guys go upstairs? I'll be up in a minute."

Still white-faced, the man nodded, and led the family to the stairs. But they hadn't yet moved out of earshot when Callie said with contempt, "They look like *vagrants* to me! My father's not going to like this one bit when he hears about it, Kate. Med Center isn't a charitable organization."

Kate saw Mr. Sloan's back stiffen as he went up the stairs. She knew he'd heard. Annie probably had, too. Fury shook Kate's hands. She wanted to slap Callie, but she held back.

Shaking his head in disgust, Eddie closed the door and went back to his duties.

"Listen," Kate hissed heatedly, "you didn't have to embarrass those people that way. What's it to you if a few slices of meat loaf and some mashed potatoes don't make it into the garbage disposal?"

"They *are* vagrants, aren't they?" Callie declared triumphantly. "I *knew* it!" She tossed her head. "They've got no business here. There are shelters for people like that."

Kate fumed. "On a night like this, every shelter in the city was full hours ago."

Callie shrugged. "Then your *friends* should have gone there hours ago instead of hanging around here." Her voice hardened. "If I see them here again, I'm calling security. My father has enough on his mind tonight without worrying about people like that coming in here, bringing disease and germs with them." Callie's thin upper lip curled in distaste as she added, "They looked . . . unclean."

Kate gave up. "Yeah, well," she said, turning away toward the stairs, "it's probably a little tough shampooing when you don't own a home with a shower anymore. And it's kind of cold tonight to be taking baths in the Revere River, right, Callie?"

Behind her, Callie sniffed disdainfully.

Kate went on upstairs.

When she reached the waiting room, there was no sign of the Sloan family.

They were gone.

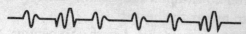

In the trauma room where the cardiac patient lay bare-chested on the table, small rubber suction cups connecting his chest to a monitor, Dr. Izbecki shook his head. A man of average height with a plain, honest face, he stood alongside the crash cart Damon had moved into the room and called for "Lidocaine, IV push!" while a nurse applied gel to the paddles from the cart.

The doctor began, "We need a chest film — " but was interrupted by a nurse shouting, "He's in fib!" Without waiting for a signal, she thrust the gelled paddles into the doctor's hands.

Kate entered the room, moving to stand beside Susannah. They had both witnessed similar scenes countless times. They knew by heart how it went. But that never made it any less scary.

Izbecki took the paddles while a nurse tended the dials that dictated how many volts of electricity were administered. "Three hundred!" the doctor ordered, and the nurse set the dial. When Izbecki shouted, "Clear!" all medical personnel stepped away from the table. Then the doctor slammed the charged paddles down upon the victim's chest in an effort to restart the heart.

Susannah held her breath. Sometimes this procedure worked on the first try, other times it took repeated efforts, with the voltage being upped each time. Sometimes it didn't work at all, the only result a continuing flat line on the monitor that was disheartening to see.

But usually, it worked.

It worked this time, and to everyone's relief, it only took two attempts.

A collective sigh of relief whispered around the room as the monitor began to indicate a sinus rhythm, which meant a regular heartbeat.

Damon, waving at Kate, left to rejoin his unit. Kate resisted the feeling of disappointment she always suffered when Damon left, especially if they hadn't had a chance to talk, or to kiss good-bye.

But this was much too busy a night to be thinking about things like that. She'd see him later.

Besides, she had the Sloan family on her mind. Where *were* they?

Kate glanced around the trauma room. This

patient was out of danger. And there was more than enough medical staff here to look after him. She slipped silently out of the room.

"Okay, Donald," Dr. Izbecki said sternly to the man, who was fully conscious, "you know what they say. Three strikes and you're out. This was your third cardiac episode. You don't get another chance, you read me? No more shoveling snow. Spend a few bucks and hire someone to do it. Or let the snow bury your house, before we have to bury *you*. You are not going to get lucky a fourth time, I promise you that. I'm sending you upstairs to see Barlow again before you leave here. This time, do what he tells you to, okay? And you're going to pay a fortune for his advice, so don't ignore it."

Abby was waiting outside the trauma room when Susannah and Will emerged. "You had a code? I heard someone shouting, 'Clear.' So I knew something was going on. Heart attack?"

Susannah nodded. "He's going to be okay, though. Izbecki reamed him. I think the patient probably got the message this time."

"We're going to have more cardiacs," Will said flatly as they made their way down a hall cluttered with metal supply carts, unoccupied gurneys, and empty wheelchairs. "The snow is coming down thick and fast now. Everybody and his brother will be out there playing macho man with a shovel, guys whose only other exercise all year is surfing the remote from their recliners."

Abby agreed. "The wind is wild. I could hear it howling around the building when I was in X ray. It sounded like a siren." She led the way to the nurses' station. Kate was there, leaning against the counter. She glanced up when they arrived, but said nothing.

"So," Susannah addressed Abby, "what else is going on? Anything new in the last twenty minutes?"

Abby began ticking cases off on her fingers. "Three more car wrecks, no fatalities. Another cardiac. Two pregnancies. They were taken straight upstairs to ob-gyn. The worst case was this couple was coming home from getting groceries. One of their kids had left a bicycle in the driveway, so the husband let the woman out to move it before he drove on into the garage. She got the bike and moved it out of the way, but then she slipped on the ice. She slid right underneath the car. Her husband didn't see it happen. He thought she was on the lawn. The wheels ran right over her when he stepped on the gas. Crushed her chest. Dr. Mulgrew had to put a tube in, and then they rushed her upstairs to surgery."

Susannah thought of the husband, who had

to be horrified by the accident, and she shuddered.

"And," Abby added grimly, "I haven't heard a word from Sid. Still haven't been able to reach his mother, either. I guess some of the phone lines *are* down, although ours are still working." She turned to Will. "Don't the Rehab vans have cellular phones? I mean, you would think they would, since some of the people who use them would be in a real fix if they got stranded. They'd need to call someone, right?"

"Right. But I don't have a clue if the vans are equipped with phones. Why don't you call Rehab and ask?"

Abby did that. When she put the phone down, her dark eyes were bleak. "Some of the vans have phones. But," she looked at Susannah, tears shining in her eyes, "not Sid's. Not the one he borrowed tonight. And Rehab hasn't heard from him 'either. They expected him an *hour* ago."

"Don't worry about Costello," Will said heartily. "He survived a fall from the water tower, didn't he? He'll survive this blizzard, too, O'Connor, bet on it." He began to move away, but as he did so, he caught Susannah's eye and tilted his head, indicating that she should come with him.

She was reluctant to leave Abby, but she wanted to know what Will had to say to her. She needed to talk to him, too, and this was the first chance they'd had all evening.

Telling Abby she'd be right back, Susannah followed Will to a dim corner near the front entrance. The waiting room to their left was crowded. Almost every chair was full now. The people inside were watching the weather channel. Susannah caught a glimpse of a large area of green surrounding the city of Grant. Odd, she thought, that green should symbolize snow.

"Oh, man," Will muttered, following Susannah's gaze, "it's getting worse. You really think Sid is out there somewhere?"

"Maybe not. Maybe he's safe at his mother's house. I hope." She turned away from the door to lean against the wall, facing Will. It was cold in the lobby, and it smelled strongly of antiseptic. Susannah wondered if the smell scared incoming patients. "I know Abby would really freak out if something happened to Sid. I mean, something worse than what's already happened to him."

Will leaned against the opposite wall. "I'd go look for him if I wasn't on duty."

Susannah felt a flutter of alarm. "The vans are white. They'll be hard to spot tonight, maybe even impossible. You could end up getting lost out there yourself."

His voice was light, but his eyes on hers were serious. "And that would make you feel . . . ?"

She spoke firmly. "That would make me feel lousy, Will Jackson, and you know it."

He crossed the wet tile in three long strides and, placing an arm on the wall on each side of her, looked down into her face. "Would you come looking for *me* if I got lost in a snowstorm?"

Susannah wasn't smiling when she returned his gaze. "Only if you promise right this minute to never, ever push me into a date with someone else again. What a stupid idea! *I'll* decide if I want to date someone else."

"That ticked you off?" Will grinned, feigning surprise. "Jeez, the guy is rich, he's going to make even bigger bucks as an MD, and he looks like he belongs on the cover of a magazine. You sure are hard to please."

"Yes, I am." Susannah told herself she shouldn't forgive him so quickly. She'd been really hurt and angry when he'd pushed her on Alec Blackstone. But no one in the waiting room was paying any attention to them, and there was no one in the lobby. They had so little time alone together. "I am very hard to please." She reached up to put her arms around his neck, and she was smiling. "I have had only the best all of my life, remember. Why should I settle for a self-involved, narcissistic egomaniac like Alec Blackstone when I can have an opinionated, stubborn, hardheaded fool like Willis Tyler Jackson?"

He bent his head to lay his cheek against hers. "Opinionated?" he murmured, taking his hands from the wall to place them around her waist and pull her close. Then he reached down and lifted her face to his. "Stubborn? Hardheaded? *Fool*?"

"Yep," Susannah murmured, closing her eyes. "All of the above. I don't know *what* I see in you."

"Me, either," he said. Then he kissed her, and he put into the kiss all of the things he couldn't say aloud . . . I'm sorry I was such an idiot, I'm sorry I hurt you, I'm sorry I made you mad. What the kiss *didn't* say was, And I'll never do it again. But then, Susannah hadn't expected to hear that.

She'd worry about that later. Right now, she wanted one more kiss before they parted. And she got it, just before another ambulance call pulled the two of them apart.

As Will turned to hurry away, Susannah called, "I know who would be perfect for your friend, Alec Blackstone."

Will stopped, glancing over his shoulder. "Who?"

"Who else? Callie Matthews. If she forgot her mirror, he could lend her his."

Will was still laughing when he rounded a corner and disappeared.

chapter
11

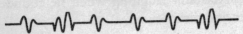

At the nurses' station, waiting for her next assignment, Abby turned to Kate. "I just remembered. You said you needed to talk to me. What about?"

Kate explained about the Sloan family. "Now they're out there in the blizzard somewhere, probably freezing to death," she finished. "You said you wanted to be a social worker, right? So, I thought maybe you could help. If we can find them, where exactly should the Sloans go for help?"

Abby thought for a minute. "Isn't there a hotline in Grant for homeless people? You could try that. But," she added dubiously, "that probably just tells where in town the shelters are. And I'll bet anything they're full tonight."

"That's what I tried to tell Callie. She was freaking out because I gave food to the Sloans. You'd think I'd stolen the food right out of her mouth! I was hoping the family would come back here for the night. But if Callie tells her father, he'll alert security to keep an eye out for them and kick them to the curb the minute they show up here."

"I don't see why they can't stay," Abby said. "They're not hurting anyone, sitting in the waiting room. We could probably find some place better after things calm down a little." She sighed. "I know we're having a tiny little lull now, but it won't last. Later on, maybe we can find an empty room . . ."

"An empty room for what?" Lily Dolan asked as, popping the top on a cold can of soda, she joined them. Most of her left cheekbone was decidedly purple, with a hint of yellow in the center.

Kate whistled under her breath. "That's some shiner," she said. "What'd you do, walk into a door?"

Abby jabbed her in the ribs with an elbow. Startled, Kate grunted, shooting Abby a look of annoyed surprise.

"Something like that," Lily answered, shrugging. "I repeat, what do you need an empty room for?"

Kate was willing to share information about the Sloans only with people who might be able to help. Lily couldn't help. If Lily Dolan knew how to help families in trouble, she wouldn't be sporting an angry bruise on her cheek. If she knew where people in trouble went to find safety, she'd have left the Dolan house long ago.

Kate understood then why Abby had elbowed her. Because she knew that Lily hadn't walked into any "door." Lily had walked into her father's fist. It probably hadn't been the first time, either.

Trying to hide her disgust with Tommy Dolan, Kate said quietly, "Forget it, Lily."

Lily glanced from Abby to Kate and back again. "Wow, what is up with you two?" Uneasiness filled her eyes. "My father hasn't been around, has he? Looking for me? Is that what you don't want to tell me?"

The uneasiness was contagious. Kate and Abby exchanged another glance, this one saying, Oh, great! The last thing we need in the ER tonight is a drunken Tommy Dolan. "No," Abby answered, "we haven't seen him. If he shows up, should we tell him you're not here?"

"It wouldn't do any good. He knows I'm on duty." Lily's fingers went to her cheek again. "I have this weird feeling that he'll pop up. With the roads the way they are, he just might be carted in on a gurney." She finished her soda in one long swallow. "The man's a menace on the highway even on a good night." As she turned and hurried away, she called over her shoulder, "If you see him — and he's still breathing — tell him I left, okay?"

There was a prolonged silence after she'd gone. Then Abby said quietly, "She didn't mean that. If her father was hurt, she'd help take care of him, I know she would."

Kate wasn't so sure. The bruise on Lily's cheek was a really nasty one. The blow that caused it must have been vicious. Maybe Lily wasn't willing to forgive this time.

If I can find out where people like the Sloans go to be safe, Kate told herself, maybe I'll mention it to Lily, in case she needs to go there, too.

When Susannah and Will returned from the lobby, Kate told them about the Sloans. Maybe Susannah's father could help in some way. Will might know something about available shelters. But first, the missing family had to be found.

It was Will's idea to send Sam in search of the Sloans. "With the wind throwing a tantrum out there, Sam's wasting his time shoveling. The snow blows right back in his face. If he does make any headway, he'll just be uncovering the ice. That's not such a great idea. Why not ask him to hunt for your missing family? He could have seen them leave. Maybe he noticed which way they went."

Abby looked skeptical. "Sam? I've never thought of him as a knight in shining armor."

Susannah bristled. "Abby, that's not fair!

Sam hasn't had much chance to be a hero, except on an athletic field. I think he'll do this, if Kate tells him how important it is." To Kate, she said, "Just explain that the family must be freezing in their thin jackets. You have to describe to him what they were wearing, anyway, so he'll recognize them when he sees them. Make sure you tell him there are three little kids."

An ambulance call sounded over the PA system, and Will took off.

Kate turned to Susannah. "You come with me. I hardly know Sam. You're his sister, he'll listen to you."

"Oh, you think he'll listen to me, do you?" Susannah responded sarcastically.

But she put her coat on and followed Kate outside.

Sam was still there. He had worked his way out from underneath the canopy, and was nearly hidden from view within a swirling cocoon of white. His bare head and dark brown suede bomber jacket were thick with snow, as if they'd been frosted. He seemed completely involved in the battle to keep the ambulance driveway clear. His handsome face was flushed with exertion and windburn, but he shoveled with ease, as if this were the sort of activity he engaged in every day.

Susannah regarded him with awe. Sam

never did chores like this at home. Of course, she reminded herself, no one ever asked him to.

Susannah wondered if her brother would like to be asked to help at home, once in a while. Maybe he needed to feel useful. *Only* once in a while, of course. If performing chores became a regular thing, Sam would become disenchanted very quickly. He never stuck to any one thing . . . any one *girl*, especially . . . for any length of time. But he seemed almost to be having fun now.

And she saw a light appear in his eyes when Kate explained why a search for the family was necessary. Totally undaunted by the vicious wind ripping at his scalp, Sam nodded eagerly, listening carefully to Kate's description of what the Sloans looked like and what they had been wearing.

He *wants* to help Kate, Susannah realized. Why was she surprised? Sam loved adventures, and that was probably how he saw Kate's request. Didn't he realize that venturing out into the storm could be dangerous?

"There can't be too many families wandering around in this," he said heartily, tossing his shovel aside. "I'll go on foot. It'll be faster that way, considering what kind of shape the roads are in. How long ago did they leave? They were walking, too, right?"

"I don't know," Kate answered honestly. "They must have been. If they had a car, they'd probably be living in it. They wouldn't be able to make very good time, not with three kids. They should still be around here somewhere. But you're going to have to really *look* for them, Sam. I'd guess the first thing they did when they left here was look for another place to get out of the storm. They might have taken refuge in a maintenance shed or in one of the other hospitals in the complex. They could be anywhere."

Sam nodded. "Gotcha. I'll find them." Pulling his jacket collar up around his ears and hunching his shoulders against the wind, Sam set off on foot.

"Maybe he should have taken someone else with him," Kate wondered aloud, watching him go. "There is probably a good reason why rescue workers always travel in teams. You can't see more than a few inches in this! He could get lost."

"Sam's lived in Grant all of his life." Susannah shivered with cold in spite of her heavy jacket. "He won't get lost."

But she sounded more certain than she felt. This was Massachusetts, where winter storms could be deadly. She'd heard stories of people who lived in the country getting lost walking from their home to their barn in a bad storm.

If someone could get lost and freeze to death in the snow only a few hundred feet from his or her own home, how could she be positive that the same thing wouldn't happen to her brother?

Susannah was thinking, I should have gone with him, when an ambulance raced up the driveway. At the same time, Dr. Santiago, a tall, burly-chested man in a gray coat, came hurrying out of the building. Astrid, two orderlies, and a nurse named Peggy, were right behind him. They had clearly been expecting this new arrival.

"Time to get back to work," Kate murmured.

Sending one last, worried glance after her brother and finding that he had completely vanished into the storm, Susannah turned toward the ambulance.

Later, when he heard about what happened, Sam would say it was his fault. If he hadn't shoveled the snow off the driveway, he would say, the ice would still have been buried, and the ambulance, traveling at a fast clip, wouldn't have hit the clear, glossy spot in the center of the driveway.

But Susannah disagreed. It wasn't Sam's fault. Watching, she could tell exactly when the driver made his mistake. The ambulance began its sideways slide, and she knew just what he was going to do. He wanted to stop the dizzying slide of his ambulance, and letting his instincts take over, he did what he had always done to stop a moving vehicle: He stomped down hard on the brake.

The result was exactly the opposite of what the driver intended. The abrupt braking intensified the spinning motion. The vehicle spun around, full circle, once, then a second time, completely out of control now, while the crowd under the canopy stared in horror.

The ambulance continued to spiral rapidly toward the crowd. He won't dare hit the brakes again, Susannah thought, her pulse racing. How was the vehicle ever going come to a stop?

Very quietly, Dr. Santiago said, "I believe that we must all go inside."

Because of the calming effect of his voice, no one panicked. But what they all heard in that voice was, *we are all in danger*.

Santiago turned, yanked the door open. He motioned to Astrid to precede him into the building. Susannah, behind Kate, turned to look over her shoulder again, and gasped when she saw how fast the ambulance was coming. It was unmistakeably headed, now, straight for the group hurrying out of its path.

The last person, orderly Joey Rudd, stepped

inside. The ambulance wheels hit the bare ice underneath the canopy, and spun around one more time. It was hurtling backward when it crashed into the side of the building just beyond the double doors.

It hit with enough force to knock out most of the exterior wall. Bricks flew in every direction. There were screams and cries from the small group of people who had just taken refuge inside the building.

More startled cries came from people in the waiting room who heard the horrendous sounds but could not yet see what was happening.

The ambulance, slowed by the collision with the brick wall, plowed on into the emergency lobby another twenty-five feet or so, knocking aside medical carts and splintering wheelchairs and taking with it half a dozen blue plastic chairs that had been lining the wall.

It finally came to a halt against a wall that housed four giant vending machines, shattering the glass doors of every one. There was a startled cry of pain, but in the midst of so much noise, it was impossible to identify the source of the cry.

Cellophaned packages of peanut-buttered crackers and tiny boxes of raisins and small, brightly colored envelopes of candies flooded to the floor. Cans of soda spilled out, rolling and rattling along the tile. Showers of coins poured from the machines, spinning crazily when they landed.

Finally, everything stopped.

chapter

12

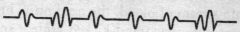

After several moments of stunned silence, the lobby came to life again. When it did, chaos took over.

People with open magazines still in their hands rushed from the waiting room to see what had happened. Nurses, doctors, and orderlies in white or gray or green ran to the scene. Commanding shouts and cries of alarm rang out as disbelieving eyes took in the wreckage the ambulance had created. Blowing snow and frigid air poured in through the yawning hole in the brick wall.

Susannah had thrown herself to the floor a split second before the ambulance roared into the building. For several minutes after the crash, she lay on the cold, wet tile, too dazed to move. She could see Astrid opposite her, climbing to her feet, apparently unharmed. The head nurse glanced around, as if she were trying to get her bearings.

A number of rubber-soled feet rushed past

Susannah. She felt that she should move, but her muscles seemed incapable of motion.

She saw Dr. Santiago check quickly to see if Astrid had suffered any injuries. There was a small cut just below her left eye. Swiping at the thin stream of blood, the head nurse broke away from Santiago and kicked aside a splintered wooden chair to make her way toward the ambulance. "Where is Kate?" Susannah heard her ask.

Someone kept repeating in a loud voice, "Is anybody hurt? Is anybody hurt?" It sounded like Lily Dolan's voice.

Susannah heard cries of pain, too. She hoped they were coming from suture or treatment rooms, not from somewhere near her. Because if the cries of pain were here, in the lobby, that would mean someone had been hurt in the crash.

I have to get up, she thought. But her head felt so fuzzy, she stayed where she was. She didn't feel ready to see if her body still worked properly.

Her second reaction was indignation at how noisy it was in the lobby. This is a hospital, she thought angrily. What is all that racket? Don't they know patients are trying to sleep? Sick people need their rest. *Who* is making all that noise?

If she had been asked, she would have said

she was experiencing a perfectly reasonable reaction to all the noise and confusion. It wouldn't be until much later that she would remember being angry about the noise and think, How silly.

An arm in a navy blue sleeve reached down to help her to her feet. Surprised, she looked up and saw Will. He was looking down at her with concern in his eyes.

When she was standing, he kept his arm around her waist, waiting for Susannah to steady herself.

"I'm not hurt," she said shakily. But she leaned against him slightly because her knees felt like pudding. "Where did you come from?"

"You sure you're not hurt? You've got a lump on your forehead the size of an ostrich egg." Will led her to a chair and gently deposited her there. Her back was to the ambulance. "I just got back from a call. False alarm. We thought it was a cardiac case, but it was just indigestion. We didn't even bring the guy in." Will remained standing, and if Susannah thought it was odd that he was talking so much, she dismissed the thought because *everything* seemed so odd just then. "We saw the mess when we pulled in the driveway. Couldn't figure out what had happened. When we got inside, Santiago explained." Will let out a heavy sigh. "What a mess! What about that bump? You could have a concussion."

Susannah shook her head. It was beginning to clear. "I'm fine. Where's Kate?" She tried to search with her eyes, but Will was still firmly positioned between her and the crash scene. The rest of the lobby was thick with onlookers, staff, and maintenance personnel scooping up debris. It was difficult to tell one person from another, but Susannah saw no sign of Kate's brightly colored dashiki. "Have you seen her? She was outside with me. She should be right here somewhere."

Will had fallen strangely silent. When she looked up at him questioningly, he avoided her eyes. "Come on," he said quietly, reaching down to take her hand. "Let's get Izbecki or Lincoln to take a look at that bump, okay?"

There was something about his voice. It was too quiet, too calm, considering what was going on around them. "Will?" Susannah tried to peer around him, to see what was going on against the side wall, where the emergency vehicle was parked backward. "Will, where is Kate?"

Two firemen burst through the rear doors, glancing only momentarily at the shattered wall as they entered. One of the men, in black slicker, helmet and boots, was Damon Lawrence. Susannah turned sideways on her chair to watch as Abby ran up to Damon and began speaking earnestly.

Damon's dark eyes widened in shock. He broke into a run toward the crowd gathered around the ambulance.

"What did Abby say to him?" Susannah asked Will. "Why is he here? He's a fireman. Is the ambulance leaking gasoline?" She sniffed the air. She didn't smell anything except the normal medicinal odor of the hospital.

"No. No gas leak." Kneeling in front of her, Will said quietly, "Okay, this is dumb. You should know what's going on. Just don't get upset, okay? It's not as bad as it looks. It'll be fine, I promise."

Susannah tried to sort out his words. *What* would be fine? Why was he telling her not to get upset? How could she not be upset? Wasn't *everyone* upset by what had just happened? "Will? What's going on that I don't know about?"

There was a loud, angry cry from somewhere behind her and this time, Susannah knew it wasn't coming from a suture room. It was coming from right there in the lobby. From right . . . over . . . there . . .

Her head turned, and at that moment, the crowd parted to let the firemen in, and Susannah saw what Will didn't want her to see. She saw sneakered feet poking out from beneath the ambulance. The jeans had inched up just enough to reveal a glimpse of bright yellow socks.

All of the volunteers except one wore white socks or tights, or sometimes pink to match their smocks. Kate chose brighter colors, to match the vivid tones in her dashikis.

That was Kate Thompson lying underneath the ambulance.

Susannah's hands flew to her mouth. "Oh, no," she whispered, "oh, no! Is she . . . is she . . . ?"

"She's fine," Will said hastily, squeezing Susannah's hand. "She's been talking to us." He laughed lightly as he stood up. "She says she feels like that witch in *The Wizard of Oz* when the house landed on her."

Susannah stood up, too. "How could she not be hurt?"

"Looks like she threw herself to the floor when you did, and the thing ran right over her. I mean just that. *Over* her. The tires never touched her. But she's stuck."

"Stuck?"

"Her right arm is pinned between the wall and the back of the ambulance."

Susannah looked alarmed. "Is the arm broken? I heard her crying out a few minutes ago. She sounded like she was in pain."

"She's just mad. I don't think anything's

broken. They're trying to drive the thing out of here, but the engine died. They can't get it going."

"I don't care about the ambulance," Susannah said, beginning to move forward. "I'm just worried about Kate. I don't believe she's okay. How could she be?"

"Izbecki checked her out. He said she's not bleeding, and although he can't be sure yet, he didn't think anything was broken. He said her pulse is just a little accelerated. BP is fine, too. He thinks she's more mad than hurt. Scared, too, probably. But he agrees, they need to get her out of there, so we can be sure she's okay."

Susannah saw Astrid standing near the rear of the ambulance, against the shattered vending machines, her eyes on the floor where her daughter lay hidden from her. The cut over the head nurse's eye was still bleeding, but she seemed unaware of it.

Will and Susannah watched in silence for several moments as the ambulance driver climbed back into the vehicle and made another futile attempt at starting the engine. It made no sound at all, not so much as a chug or cough.

Glancing around, she asked Will if anyone else had been hurt. She saw no one lying injured on the floor. Most of the staff seemed to be working to clear debris. Lily was standing with Astrid, talking calmly to Kate, and Abby had just left the crowd around the ambulance and was making her way over to Susannah and Will. "Does anyone here have broken bones?"

"Leo, one of the paramedics in the ambulance. He was slammed against the passenger's window when they hit that brick wall. If they'd been traveling forward instead of backwards, he'd have been hurt a lot worse. I think his nose is broken, and he's probably got a concussion, too. Dr. Lincoln and a couple of nurses already got him out of here. I should go see how he is."

"Who was driving?"

"Joel Mitchum. I think Leo's probably pretty ticked at him, though, for hitting that driveway at top speed. Joel should have slowed down."

Susannah's knees steadied. But she continued to lean against Will. She felt safe there, safe from the noise and confusion and the cold wind blowing in through the shattered wall.

Damon had crawled beneath the ambulance and was working to free Kate's arm. Susannah couldn't tell if he was having any luck.

"No one in the lobby was injured?"

"Bruises and scrapes." Will pointed to the nurse named Peggy and one of the orderlies who had been outside, now being helped away from the scene by other orderlies and nurses.

Peggy's cheek was bloody. The orderly was holding his left arm gingerly. "That seems to be the worst of it." Will gave her a hug, saying, "Gotta tell you, though, looks like the vending machines are in critical condition. Probably not much hope for them."

Susannah didn't laugh. She couldn't take her eyes off Kate's feet. For some reason, the bright yellow socks were reassuring.

Although there were at least eight or ten people trying to help Kate, they didn't seem to be doing much good. Every time someone tugged on her arm, no matter how gently, she cried out. It didn't sound like an angry cry to Susannah. It sounded like a cry of pain. She winced each time she heard it.

Abby moved to stand beside Will, asking in a tremulous voice, "You okay, Sooz?"

"I think so. How about you?"

"I'm fine. Just feeling a little sick, that's all. When I came in here and saw you lying there, I thought you were dead. I thought the ambulance had hit you."

Susannah reached out to give Abby's hand a reassuring squeeze. "I know. We were all really lucky. Except for Kate. Can't someone *move* that ambulance? Tow it or something? It's the only way to get Kate out of there."

Will sent her a skeptical glance. "Every tow truck in town will be out on calls. It'd be hours before we could get one over here."

When they had moved through the crowd to the back of the ambulance, Susannah saw Damon working frantically to set Kate free. His mouth looked grim. He tried pushing against the rear of the ambulance, and when that didn't work, ordered others to do the same. When the vehicle failed to budge, the look on his face alarmed Susannah. It was a look of defeat.

According to Kate, Damon Lawrence never gave up on anything. He wasn't giving up now, was he? He couldn't. They had to get Kate out of there.

chapter
13

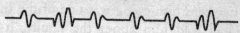

Sam Grant wasn't used to slogging through snow and ice on foot. He drove everywhere in his shiny, silver van. He had never envied Susannah the Benz. It was a cool car, but too small for his needs. He had too many friends in need of a ride to settle for a little sports car. The van was perfect.

Man, did he miss it now! He had never been so cold in his life. When he exhaled, his breath became a thick cloud of steam. His hands, bare of the leather gloves that, he remembered with regret, were lying on the front seat of the van, were frozen. And his lips were so numb, he couldn't have formed a word to save his life. He could no longer shout for the Sloans, as he'd done in the beginning, but it didn't seem to matter. He knew they wouldn't have heard him over the fierce roar of the wind.

Discouraged, Sam thought, Not only am I *not* having any luck finding that family for Kate, but I'll be lucky if I can find my own way back to the hospital. He couldn't make out a single redbrick building. Every landmark, every inch of walkway, every light pole, had disappeared, all of it obliterated by the white cocoon around him.

What kept him going was one of the things Kate had told him about the family. It was what she had said about their clothing. "All of their jackets were as thin as tissue paper," she'd said.

He was wearing a heavy, fur-lined suede jacket, and although any exposed areas were numb, the part of his body covered by the jacket was still comfortably warm. According to Kate, the five people he was searching for had no such protection. She'd been very clear about that.

The Sloan family had to be freezing. Sam realized that this was a truly dangerous storm. How could the family possible survive these temperatures and the vicious wind, in inadequate clothing?

He had to find them.

Damon Lawrence worked feverishly to free Kate. He was afraid that if she cried out one more time in pain, he was going to totally lose it. And he couldn't do her *any* good if he lost his cool.

Susannah, Abby, and Lily remained on one

side of the ambulance, talking to Kate, trying to keep her spirits up. Astrid crouched on the other side, reaching under the vehicle to hold Kate's free hand tightly in both of hers. Her face looked strained, her mouth tight with anxiety.

Damon was glad they were there. It seemed to him that Kate's voice was becoming weaker. She'd started out joking, even laughing, but had moved quickly to irritation and impatience and now, he thought, fear. He couldn't see her face. Except for the arm pinned between the wall and the vehicle, she was hidden from sight by the ambulance. But he envisioned her gorgeous dark eyes wide with fear, and the image sent a surprisingly sharp arrow of pain into his own heart.

Damon had known Kate most of his life. But it was only recently, after he'd pulled his life together, earned his GED and become a fireman, with plans to attend college next year, that they'd become close. Not as close as he'd like. Not yet. But closer than they'd been after he'd dropped out of high school to work at the refinery. He'd seldom seen Kate during that time, after seeing her constantly while they were growing up. He'd missed her, although he hadn't realized how much until he met her again at the hospital last summer.

In all the time Damon had known Kate,

he'd never seen her frightened, never seen her hurt or helpless. What blew his mind was how rotten it made him feel, knowing that she might be hurting under that ambulance. It made him almost crazy, wanting to get her out of there and make her safe. He'd never felt that way about anyone. Scary.

They argued a lot, because they were both pigheaded. When they weren't arguing, he did his part to keep the relationship cool. He knew that was what Kate wanted. She had plans, big plans, and she'd been straight with him from the start about that. She wanted to be a doctor, and no one was gong to get in her way. But now Damon had plans, too. And with a future of his own, it was easier to understand Kate's determination. So he kept things light and casual.

The way he felt now, thinking of her under this stupid, stubborn ambulance whose engine refused to start, was anything but light and casual. He'd have done anything to get her out from under there. Anything.

"You've gotta get this thing out of here," he told Joel, the driver. "Get a mechanic over here, have him fix it."

"Yeah, right." Joel shrugged. "I've tried six mechanics. All of the shops are closed. Two of the guys left home numbers on their answering machines, but they weren't there, ei-

118

ther. Probably out replacing dead batteries in stranded cars. Even if I found someone, what makes you think he could make it over here? The roads are a mess!"

Damon shot him a caustic glance. "That didn't slow *you* down, did it? I hear you thought the driveway outside was the Indy five hundred racetrack."

Joel seemed unperturbed. "I guess I should have slowed down." He glanced around the lobby. Most of the mess had been cleaned up, but the air of anxiety around the trapped girl was palpable. "Isn't there anyone here who knows his way around an engine?"

Damon *had* worked on his old pickup truck after school for hours before he'd taken the refinery job. How different could an ambulance engine be? A car was a car, and an engine was an engine.

Stripping off his raincoat and signaling to Will to come and help him, Damon rolled up the sleeves of his blue uniform shirt. He ordered Joel to flip the lever that opened the hood. Then he went to work to free Kate.

In the large, white van sitting at a tilt in the snow-filled ditch, Sid Costello fought to stay calm.

He would have killed for a cell phone. Then all he'd have to do would be pick it up, dial the hospital, give his situation and his location to whoever answered. Then he'd sit back and wait to be rescued.

But there *was* no phone.

That made Sid mad. These vans were all driven by people just like him. People who could handle life okay under normal circumstances, but who, in extraordinary circumstances, like being stranded on an unfamiliar road in the middle of a raging blizzard, needed help.

He hated that so much . . . that he needed help. He would never get used to that feeling. Abby had said that he *shouldn't* get used to it . . . that if he did, he might stop trying to do everything for himself. "Not that I'm worried," she'd added, her smile saying she knew him too well for that.

Was she worried now? Sid glanced at his illuminated watch. A little after ten . . . she'd expected him back at Emsee by nine. She knew this was his first outing in the van. She'd tried so hard not to act concerned when he left earlier that day. It had been raining, and she had glanced up at the charcoal-gray sky with an anxious look on her face.

He had to give her credit. She knew how much he hated being fussed over, so she'd put on a big act, pretending she was only worried that it might get cold, and the rain would turn to snow. Yeah, right. What she was *worried* about was that he might not be able to handle the van if the roads got bad.

And she'd been right, hadn't she?

If she was worried now, she might send someone out to look for him. The problem was, he was pretty sure now that he had taken a wrong turn somewhere. He was lost. Since *he* had no idea where he was, how could anyone find him? They'd be looking for him in an entirely different part of the city.

Maybe someone would come along.

What good would that do? No one would spot a white van in the middle of a blinding blizzard. It was pitch-black out here. No houses that he could see, and no streetlights. If he left his headlights on in the hope that someone would spot the faint glow, the battery would die. He couldn't let that happen. He might need the heater at some point, if he didn't want to freeze to death.

But turning on the engine to use the heater could be dangerous. He had no way of knowing whether or not the van's tailpipe was in the clear. It could be buried in snow. If it was, and he turned on the engine, fumes from the exhaust would back up into the car's interior, spreading a deadly poison that would kill him.

Sid laughed, a loud, harsh sound that bounced off the walls of the van. One of the things he hated about being partially paralyzed was that it limited his choices. He didn't like having his choices limited. Even after months of recuperation and rehabilitation, it burned like acid when he couldn't do something he'd done before the accident.

But never, not once since he'd fallen from that stupid tower, had his choices been as dangerously limited as they were now.

chapter
14

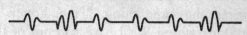

It took Damon and Will twenty minutes to find the problem in the disabled engine and fix it. They were twenty very long minutes for Kate, her mother, and her friends.

Especially Kate. She wondered if Sam had had any luck finding the Sloans. He should have been back by now. How long had she been under this stupid ambulance, anyway? Would she *ever* get out?

Of course she would. Damon would get her out. When he'd peered under the ambulance to look in at her, she'd seen his eyes full of fierce determination, as if he had every intention of lifting the heavy ambulance off her with his bare hands.

But there was something else in Damon's eyes, too, Kate thought. Sadness? No, more than sadness. Pain? Maybe pain. Had Damon's eyes looked that way because of her?

Her pinioned arm burned. She had an uneasy feeling that a bone might have been broken. Maybe in the wrist? There had been a nasty cracking sound when the ambulance had lurched forward. And there was too much pain for a simple bruising or a sprain.

Her mother kept taking her pulse. Every time Kate called out to ask how it was, Astrid answered the same thing. "Fine, honey. Just fine. Don't worry. We'll have you out of there in a minute."

But by now, so many minutes had passed, that last phrase didn't mean much.

Life hadn't stopped at Med Center just because Kate Thompson was trapped under an ambulance. Three more ambulances arrived, the paramedics rushing through the lobby with their gurneys without comment, as if another ambulance parked backward in the lobby was an everyday sight. Astrid refused to leave Kate, but other medical personnel, including Lily, hurried off to care for the newest patients. Susannah and Abby took turns leaving the scene to help in the treatment and trauma rooms, so that one of them would always be at Kate's side.

"If Damon gets that engine started," Kate told Susannah when Abby had run off to assist Dr. Santiago with an accident victim, "I will never argue with him again."

Susannah laughed. "Sure you will. But maybe if I go tell him that, he'll try harder."

"Judging by the expression on his face when

he started," Kate's mother commented from the other side of the ambulance, "I think that's probably unnecessary. I think he'll do whatever he has do to get this thing going again."

Suddenly, a voice called, "Lawrence, we just got a call! Fire on Thirty-second Street. It's an apartment building. C'mon, man, we gotta go!"

Kate sucked in her breath. Damon was on duty? He had to leave? But . . . but she wasn't *free* yet!

Then, Damon's voice: "I'm not going anywhere. You go ahead. I think I've found the problem here. I can't leave now."

A moment's hesitation, and then, "Lawrence, you gotta be kidding. You refuse to take a call, man, you're dead meat. Someone else can take over here."

As much as Kate wanted her freedom, she found herself urging silently, Go with him, Damon. I don't want you getting into trouble with your fire captain because of me. Go!

But she knew he wouldn't leave. She could hear it in his voice. Oh, Damon, she thought, don't do this. If you blow off the fire department, you'll never get to college. We talked about going to Grant U together, remember?

"*Go!*" Damon ordered his partner. "Take the truck. I'll get there when I can."

"What'll I tell the captain?"

"Tell him we had an emergency here and one of us had to stay and finish the job. I'll fill him in later. Go *on*, Billings."

A few minutes later, a hand reached toward her, extending a thick white towel. "Put this over your mouth and nose," Susannah's voice ordered. "To protect you from the fumes when they start the engine."

Kate obeyed. Suddenly the engine roared to life. Then the ambulance slid forward gently, no more than an inch or so. In fear of Kate's safety beneath the vehicle, Damon eased it just far enough forward to release the arm. Kate felt nothing when that happened. She wasn't even aware that it *had* happened. She didn't realize the numbed limb had dropped until the broken bone in her wrist collided with the tile. Then she knew.

She screamed once. Then she fainted.

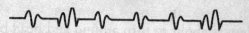

The intensity of the wind was at times helpful to Sam. Although he had to struggle against the gusts, they sporadically swept the snow aside just long enough for him to get his bearings.

The snow he was plodding through, he realized during one of these brief glimpses of his surroundings, was on Linden Boulevard. He was no longer on hospital grounds. There was no traffic. Not even a snowplow churned along beneath the huge, bare-limbed trees. The only sound was the whistling of the wind around Sam's ears, which he was valiantly trying to protect from frostbite by tugging his collar up as high as it would go.

The Sloan family wouldn't be out here, Sam told himself. They couldn't have come this far in inadequate clothing without freezing. And where would they hide out here on the boulevard?

He had come too far from Med Center. The Sloans were probably still there somewhere, taking refuge, as Kate had said, in one of the buildings. They hadn't answered any of his shouts, but if they'd heard him, they might have thought he was a cop. Or maybe they just hadn't been able to hear him over the wind.

He was about to turn around and head back to the medical complex when he spotted the car. A small sports car, so white with snow that he couldn't judge the color. When the snowplow comes along, Sam thought, it's going to bury that car.

But he had more important things on his mind than an abandoned vehicle. He would have begun his retreat then, if he hadn't suddenly noticed what looked like movement inside the car. He couldn't be sure. It was dark out, and the streetlights provided only a pale glow through the blowing snow.

He took another step closer to the stranded sports car. Though the windshield was completely blanketed with white, the passenger's window was facing into the wind, which had swept it clean. The motion came again . . . a shadowy oblong that resembled the shape of a human head. It was bobbing back and forth in a rocking motion.

Someone was inside the car.

But it made no sense. There were houses

here. If the driver was in trouble, why hadn't he gone for help?

As Sam approached the car, he tried to break into a run. His foot slipped on the ice still hidden beneath the snow, and he almost went down. His arms flailing, he regained his balance, and plodded on, as fast as he could.

When he reached the car, he brushed aside a handful of snow on the roof and peered closely at the color. A pale blue-green. Looked like the shade that Callie Matthews called "robin's-egg blue."

Of course. The size, the shape, the color . . . this was Callie's car!

But . . . Callie was at the hospital. He'd seen her there earlier. What was her car doing out here, and who was inside if it wasn't Callie?

He heard a child crying. Not too loudly, not the way a kid cries in the grocery store when it's throwing a tantrum. This crying sounded like someone was sick or hurt.

Sam bent down and stared in the window on the passenger's side. The crying had stopped. It was hard to see inside, but it looked like there was more than one person in there.

Sam rapped sharply on the glass.

The only response he received was the complete cessation of all movement inside the car.

The shadowy shape that he realized now really was a human head, only inches from his own head and separated from him by the window glass, stopped its rocking motion. But it failed to turn and acknowledge his presence.

He rapped again, harder this time. "Hey in there! You okay?"

Slowly, reluctantly, the window inched downward slightly, only an inch or so. The head he had seen was a woman's with long, dark hair. The face continued to stare straight ahead. "Yes, we're fine." The voice, though quiet, was shaking. Sam felt no heat emanating from the car's interior, and decided the shaking was probably from the cold. Why wasn't the heater on?

His eyes quickly became accustomed to the darkness inside the car. He saw a small child resting in the woman's lap, held close to her chest. Although the child wasn't crying, she let out a small, whimpering sound as icy air poured in through the open window.

There was a man sitting behind the steering wheel, next to the woman. And when Sam turned his head to inspect the rear storage compartment, he saw two pairs of eyes staring back at him.

The small child coughed, and began to cry again, a weak, plaintive cry that caused the mother to bend her head and begin stroking her cheek. "Shh," she whispered, "shh, don't cry."

Sam looked at the mother bent over the child. And he noticed, then, the clothing worn by the two adults. Even in such poor lighting, he could see that they were wearing lightweight jackets, the kind of garment you wore in the spring when the trees were leafing out and the days were warm.

He counted the passengers . . . one, two, three, four, five. There were five people sitting in Callie's stranded, robin's-egg blue sports car. Two parents, three children, and not one of them was wearing clothing suitable for a blizzard.

He had found Kate's missing family.

It was Damon who carried Kate to a treatment room. He agreed to wait outside while she was checked out by Dr. Mulgrew, but only because the doctor insisted.

When Kate had been examined and found to have no more serious injury than the broken wrist, Damon was allowed back into the room. Susannah, Will, and Abby were tactful enough to wait outside in the corridor. Dr. Mulgrew gave the pair a few minutes together before setting the wrist, and Damon and Kate were finally alone.

He bent over the table. "Got a little problem here," he said, almost whispering.

Kate was covered to the waist with a white sheet. The injured arm lay extended at her side. Someone had removed her shoes. At the end of the table, her vivid yellow socks poked out from under the edge of the sheet. Kate turned her head to look up at Damon. "So, what's the problem? Other than a broken wrist, a blizzard, a horrendous crash in the lobby, and a missing homeless family?"

Damon's eyes were very dark, almost black. "Well, see, the problem is, I gotta pick you up and hold you, Kate. I gotta see for myself that you're okay, know what I mean?"

"Well, if you're going to do that, Damon, you'd better do it right now."

He hugged her, lifting her gently to hold her close to his chest. "I thought you were history," he whispered into her hair. "When I saw those ugly yellow socks sticking out from under the ambulance, I thought it was all over. Then I heard you yell. Never thought I'd be that glad to hear you yelling, Thompson."

"Thanks for getting me out of there," Kate murmured, thinking how wonderful it felt to be held. She could feel the last trace of terror at being trapped under that ambulance disappearing in the strength of Damon's arms. "I knew you would."

"You did?" He sounded surprised.

"Yeah, I did."

Damon carefully lowered her to the table. "Look, if you feel like bawling, go ahead and let loose. Wouldn't blame you, know what I'm sayin'? Might make you feel better."

Kate looked skeptical. "Yeah, but *you'd* feel worse. Men hate it when women cry. Admit it."

Damon sighed. "You arguin' with me, after I just saved your life?"

"You didn't save my life. I wasn't dying. Or even close to dying. I was just stuck."

"Man, why do I waste my breath? You gotta be the most ungrateful . . ."

Kate interrupted by reaching up with her uninjured arm to pull his head down close to hers. "Oh, shut up, Damon," she said, before kissing him.

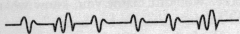

Sid knew the van's engine was working. He'd tried it several times. That wasn't the problem. The problem was, the van didn't move an inch when he put it in gear and stepped on the gas. He needed a tow truck to pull him out of the ditch.

The storm hadn't eased at all. If anything, it was worse. The snow continued to spin and swirl around him in thick sheets, like ghostly apparitions.

Because his only other choice was freezing to death in the front seat of the Rehab van, Sid finally took a chance and turned the engine on again. He waited a few more minutes before turning on the heater. How would he know if carbon monoxide was being pumped into the car's interior by a blocked exhaust pipe?

Would he be able to smell it? He didn't think so. Hadn't he once read about a family traveling in a station wagon who had arrived at their destination to find all three of their children dead? They'd been asleep in the back, and while they were sleeping, the deadly fumes had snaked into the car through a small hole in the floorboards. No one had smelled it then. So he wouldn't be able to smell it now, either.

But at the moment, Sid thought almost anything seemed better than the icy chill permeating the car . . . and *him*.

He'd just have to pay attention. If he started feeling sleepy or got a bad headache, he'd know that fumes were circulating around him, and he'd switch off the heater immediately.

At first, the air blowing out at him from the vents was chilly. He was tempted to turn the heater off, thinking it wasn't going to do him any good. But it warmed quickly.

Sid embraced the warmth, rubbing his cold hands together directly in front of one of the vents, letting the air hit his face and neck. It felt so good, he leaned his head back against the seat and let it wash over him. He would only leave it on for a few minutes.

Just long enough to wipe this terrible iciness off his bones.

He hadn't realized how tired he was until he lay his head back. It had been a long day, filled with the excitement of his first trip, his first attempt at driving any distance, his first visit home on his own. Then the weather had betrayed him, and he'd lost his way.

Now he was so tired . . .

Kate refused to leave the hospital. "I'm fine," she insisted when Astrid suggested that she go home and go to bed. "Okay, so one of my wrists has a cast on it. So what? I still have one good arm. I promise I won't try to lift anything heavier than a piece of paper. I'll just keep busy talking to patients' relatives."

"All right, if you insist," Astrid agreed reluctantly. "I don't know how you'd get home, anyway, now that I think about it. The shuttle buses have quit running, and you'd never get a taxi tonight. But if you start feeling shaky, you go lie down in the lounge, you hear me?"

"Sure. No problem." Kate didn't add that she wasn't willing to leave the hospital until Sam returned with the Sloans. The less her mother knew about her involvement with the homeless family, the better. It wasn't that she wouldn't understand. She would. But she'd insist that Kate go through "the proper channels," and that could take forever.

Kate wasn't thinking about how the family would manage in the long run. That would be up to social workers or something. All she cared about now was getting the Sloans out of the blizzard and keeping them warm and dry.

Returning to the lobby to see how the cleanup was coming along, Kate arrived just as Joel was finally driving the ambulance back outside. He was steering it straight through the gaping hole in the wall.

It was a bizarre sight.

Now there's something you don't see every day, Kate thought as she joined Will, Abby, and Susannah. They were standing off to one side, watching. Remembering the feeling of being pinned beneath the ambulance, Kate shuddered involuntarily.

"You're not going home?" Susannah asked when Kate arrived. "Your mother said — "

"She changed her mind." Kate gestured toward the ambulance. "I thought it would be long gone. How come it's just leaving now? What took so long?"

"They had to wait for the police to fill out an accident report," Will explained. "Something about insurance. Matthews got here right after Damon carted you off. You should have seen his face!"

"And Callie didn't help," Abby said. "She kept yanking on her father's arm and shouting, 'Who did this, who did this?' Like she thought someone had done it on purpose."

Remembering the ugly confrontation downstairs between Callie and the Sloan family,

Kate made a face of distaste. "That sounds like her," was all she said. But she was thinking that if Callie could have, she probably would have blamed the shattered wall on the homeless family.

When the ambulance had disappeared into the snowstorm, maintenance men armed with giant-sized sheets of heavy plastic marched toward the gap in the wall. Orderlies carrying boxes of common table salt were right behind them.

"They're going to spread the salt over the ice," Will explained. "It'll melt it. Someone should have done it hours ago. Then this wouldn't have happened. I guess they were hoping the snow would blanket the slick spots."

Susannah had been flexing the fingers of one hand tentatively. She had slammed it against something when she dropped to the floor. She didn't think anything was broken. Just bruised, but it was hurting more now than it had immediately after the accident. Her thoughts turned to her brother. "Where is Sam? Is he back yet?" she asked anyone who cared to listen.

"I haven't seen him," Will said. "If he was back, he'd be with us."

"So would Sid," Abby said, her voice suddenly gone flat. "If he were anywhere on the grounds, he'd be right here with me, checking things out. I'm going to go call his mother again." She left, shivering when she passed close to the hole in the wall where the maintenance men were working.

Kate left to see if anyone in the crowded waiting room needed help.

Susannah and Will watched in silence for several minutes as the workmen struggled to staple the heavy sheets of plastic in place. They were fighting an intense battle with the wind and snow.

"I'd better go give them a hand," Will said. "You sure you're okay?"

"I'm fine. Go ahead." Almost as an afterthought, Susannah said, "I wonder what's taking Sam so long. The Sloan family couldn't have gone that far. He should have found them by now, and brought them back here."

Will gave her a quick hug, said, "I'll be right back," and hurried over to help the maintenance men.

Susannah tried to remind herself how lucky they had all been. But it didn't work. She was too worried about Sam.

When Abby finally got through to Sid's mother, she listened with a sinking heart as

Mrs. Costello said, "Oh, he left here a long time ago, dear. He must be back at Rehab by now. Did you call over there?"

Abby didn't want to alarm the woman. A widow for years, Sid's mother lived alone. There wasn't anyone in the house to comfort her if she panicked. And she'd already been through so much since Sid's accident.

Besides, Abby told herself, Sid had probably stopped somewhere to grab a hamburger or half a dozen slices of pizza. If they didn't work him so hard in Rehab, he'd weigh two thousand pounds by now. Instead, his upper body was solid muscle.

"Oh, I forgot," Abby said hastily into the telephone. "I was thinking Sid was staying overnight at your house. But I remember now, he did say he was coming back here."

There was a moment of silence before Mrs. Costello asked, "You're at the hospital, Abby? I thought you were calling from home." Then, "If you're at Med Center, why isn't Sid with you?"

Oops, big mistake, Abby scolded herself silently. I couldn't keep my big mouth shut. "Oh, I'm working in ER tonight, Mrs. Costello. I haven't been over to Rehab at all. We're so busy here. Lots of accidents." Oh, that's right, toss out the word "accident" when the woman's son just might have had one.

Brilliant, Abigail. Shut up now. Say good-bye. "I'll call over there and talk to Sid. Thanks, Mrs. Costello. 'Bye."

She thought she had recovered well enough that Sid's mother wouldn't worry, but she couldn't be sure. All she could do was hope.

She did call Rehab. But she knew with a nagging sixth sense that Sid wasn't going to be there, knew it even before Kathy, one of his therapists, said, "Nope, he's not back yet. But a lot of the roads have been closed, Abby. He might have had to take a detour. I'll have him call you the minute he shows up, I promise."

Replacing the receiver, Abby couldn't shake her uneasiness. She knew Sid would hate it if he thought she was worried. He'd think she didn't have any faith in him.

She *did* have faith in Sid. He could do anything. In spite of his lifeless legs, he'd managed to save a little boy's life during the refinery fire, using his upper body strength to shinny up a tree and urge the youngster back down to safety. And then, even more amazingly, Sid had managed to get himself back down the tree. He'd said modestly that it was because the tree bent so far out over the river that its trunk was almost parallel to the ground, which made it easy to slide down, using his arms.

But Abby had seen that tree since then, or what was left of it after the fire, and the part of the trunk remaining didn't look *that* easy to climb down. And she had two good legs.

It wasn't Sid she didn't trust. It was the weather. If the roads were clear, and the wind wasn't gusting up to thirty miles an hour, and the temperature hadn't plummeted, she wouldn't be worried at all.

Sid wasn't home. And he wasn't at Rehab. And he certainly wasn't here with her in the ER, where she wanted him to be.

Which meant, he was out *there* somewhere. Alone.

chapter
17

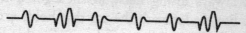

"You shouldn't be sitting here in the cold," Sam told the family in Callie's car. He knew why they hadn't gone for help. Because they believed that in this neighborhood, no one would open a door to people so shabbily dressed. Sam hoped that wasn't true. "Why don't you have the heater on? You'll freeze without it. You could crack a window if you're worried about fumes."

The adults remained mute, both staring straight ahead as if he hadn't spoken.

But then a young, defiant voice piped up from the rear. "We can't turn the heater on. It's not our car. So we don't got the keys. The door was open, though. We didn't break in or nothin'."

"We're not *stealing* it," the woman cried anxiously. "We're just sitting in it to keep warm. We saw it here, and it wasn't locked, and there wasn't anyplace else . . ."

"It's okay," Sam said, holding up a hand to stop her flow of words. He didn't want them apologizing to him. They had to be humiliated as it was, getting caught hiding out in someone else's car. "Look, I know this car. And I know where the owner keeps another key. She's always losing hers, so she's got a magnetic box underneath the car that holds extras. I'll get it. Then I'll see if I can dig this little buggy out of the snow. If I can, I'll drive all of you back to Med Center."

He heard the alarm in the woman's voice. "No, no, we can't go back there! There was this girl . . . she caught us eating . . . another girl, a nice girl, had arranged it . . . but the second girl said she was going to tell her father . . . I think he runs the place or something . . . and she said she'd call the cops on us. We can't go to jail. They'll take our kids away from us. I think my little girl is sick. Really sick, I mean. She feels warm, and she's coughing real bad. Please, can't we just stay here until she's feeling better?"

Sam shook his head. "She's not going to get any better sitting in this car. I promise you, no one's going to call the police. You have my word. Samuel Grant is my father, and if you live in this town, you must know his word is good. So is mine."

"Oh, I don't know . . ." The woman's voice was still shaking. "I'm afraid . . ."

The child in her arms whimpered again.

The mother turned away from Sam, toward her husband. "Jake?"

A deep, weary sigh. "I don't see what choice we have. She needs a doctor, Ruth."

"A doctor? We can't pay for a doctor!" the woman whispered, sounding more alarmed than before.

Overhearing, Sam felt a wash of shame. One thing he *never* worried about was money. He didn't have to. Last summer, he'd thought briefly about taking a part-time job, maybe at the refinery. He'd liked the idea of earning a few bucks on his own. It had seemed . . . adventurous, since he didn't really *have* to work.

His dad had nixed that idea real quick. He made him see that he'd have had to give up sports, dating, parties. But it was weird, though, how he'd felt kind of disappointed when he'd given up the idea.

Kate had told him this man in the car couldn't work because his arms and back had been burned in the refinery fire, that the family had lost its home to the fire, too, and had no money to rent another place. Now their kid was sick and they couldn't pay a doctor.

Sam knew he would never, never know what that felt like. His great-grandparents had been rich, his grandparents richer, his parents richer still. The longer his family lived, the more money they made. Sam was not ashamed of that. The Grants were honest people, and they gave a lot to charity. But had a single one of them ever been unable to pay a doctor?

He didn't *think* so.

Overwhelmed by a sudden, passionate need to help these people, Sam said, "I'll just get that key and dig this thing out and we'll get going, okay?"

Without waiting for an answer or an objection, Sam dropped to the ground. There was no open space under the car. It was all snow. He brushed it aside with his hands and felt for the tiny magnetic box fastened to the underbelly of the car. It took him several frozen minutes to locate it. By the time his numbed fingers brushed up against the small, ice-cold, metal box, the legs of his jeans were soaked.

"Got it!" Sam cried triumphantly, yanking the container free. He slid the top open and unearthed a key. Sam laughed quietly, thinking how ironic it was that Callie's car was going to return these people to the hospital. Kate had told him about Callie's confrontation in the kitchen with the family.

Of course, he wasn't going to tell the Sloans whose car they were sitting in. They'd be horrified. But what they didn't know couldn't hurt them.

It took Sam another ten minutes to hastily

scoop snowdrifts away from the wheels with his hands. He didn't think the car was seriously stuck. It looked to him like Callie had been going too fast, skidded on ice, and found herself hung up on the curb. She probably could have backed the thing out onto the boulevard herself if she'd been willing to try. Maybe she was worried that she'd damaged her precious sports car, running it up over the curb like that, and didn't want to try driving it, afraid she'd make things worse.

Whatever the reason, Sam was very glad she'd left the car. But she'd go ballistic when she found out the homeless family she'd chased out of Med Center had taken refuge in it.

Red-faced and breathing a little hard, Sam rapped on the driver's window. The man rolled it down.

Sam held up the ignition key. It occurred to him that the man might be feeling a little helpless right about now, what with Sam doing most of the work. "You feel like driving?" he asked, extending the key. "I'll just cram myself into the back with the kids."

The man shook his head ruefully. "I can't. I haven't driven since the fire. My back . . ."

A few minutes later, driving to Med Center, with the man squeezed uncomfortably beside his wife and the child whimpering fitfully and coughing almost constantly, Sam felt oddly happy. Content, in spite of the fact that driving was almost impossible. He could barely see, and the small car was so lightweight, even with its load of people, it slid like a toboggan whenever they hit a patch of ice. "This is a *bad* car!" the little girl in the back shouted after one particularly scary moment when they slid precariously, missing a huge tree by only inches.

Still, Sam felt great. He was *doing* something. Something good. Something useful. This was ten times better than shoveling snow. Ten times better than hosing down houses, as he'd done during the refinery fire. No matter what Callie Matthews had to say about the Sloan family, they should not be outside in this weather. No family should.

Susannah had been upstairs collecting medical supplies when she heard that a roof had collapsed on a strip shopping center just outside the city limits. "Ambulances on the way in," a nurse named Rosie Murphy informed her as Susannah emerged from a supply closet with her arms full. "You'd better get back downstairs, stat!"

The stairs were faster than the elevator. Susannah took them lightly, blonde ponytail bouncing on her shoulders, the hem of her smock flying out behind her.

When she came out of the stairwell into the lobby, a series of commands in a variety of voices sounded from the trauma, treatment, and suture rooms.

Izbecki's voice was deep and brusque. "Type and cross match, four units!"

Astrid's voice, clear and in command: "BP forty!"

Susannah heard Dr. Mulgrew's softer but equally clear tones: "Chest tube! Someone get me a chest tube, stat!"

Nurses and nurse's aides and orderlies ran from one cubicle to another, never empty-handed. They ran with blood samples to the lab, pushed gurneys upstairs to X Ray or to surgery, brought out armloads of soiled linens to dump into the laundry carts lined up against a corridor wall, and handed charts to Kate, who was standing at the nurses' station, her casted arm in a navy blue sling. She was writing with the other hand.

Susannah ran over to her. "How many injuries?" she asked hurriedly.

"Eight." Kate lifted her head. "There would have been more, but it was late, and the shopping center was closed. The people who were hurt had been stranded there when the city bus didn't show up. They were waiting outside the building, not inside, or they'd be dead now." She glanced down at a list lying on the desk. "We've got two head injuries. One's already been taken upstairs to surgery. We've got a chest injury with a collapsed lung. An iron pipe impaled this guy like a shish kebab. He was conscious when they brought him in, can you believe it?"

"Why didn't someone call me sooner?" Susannah complained.

Kate shrugged. "It wasn't necessary. One good thing about the weather, no one's been able to leave. So we've got plenty of staff." She ran an index finger down the list. "There's a fractured femur on a twelve-year-old and a broken ankle on a stock guy who was supposed to be working inside but got there late. Lucky guy. The last three were closest to the bus stop, which put them away from the building when the roof went. They've just got cuts and bruises. Ask Izbecki where he wants you, okay?"

Most of the real work had already been done when Susannah arrived to help. She was happy to just clean up and refill supply cabinets.

When she had finished, she walked to the back door to gaze out into the storm. Where was Sam? Had he found the Sloan family? Was he on his way back to Med Center with them?

A voice from behind Susannah said suddenly, "I was probably the only person in this hospital who was actually relieved to see that ambulance in the lobby."

Susannah's head swiveled. Lily Dolan moved up to stand at the door beside her.

"Relieved?" Susannah was sure she'd heard wrong. "How could you possibly be relieved?"

"When I heard about the crash, I was sure my dad had hoisted a few too many and then come here looking for me to finish our argument." Lily's voice was dry, unemotional.

Susannah had to laugh. "Lily! You didn't really think it was your father, did you?"

"Yeah, I did. He drove through our garage wall twice. Went in the front and right on out the back, taking the rear wall with him. The first time was the summer I was eleven. The second time, I was fifteen, and we never did get the wall fixed. My mother says we're the only family in town with an air-conditioned garage."

"He hit you, didn't he?" Susannah asked abruptly, her eyes on Lily's bruised cheek. "You've graduated, Lily, and you're working. Why don't you get your own place?"

"Because unlike you and your brother," Lily answered tartly, "I don't have anyone to pay my college tuition. I need to save every single penny I make, and if I had to pay rent on an apartment and buy food and pay utilities, I'd never get to college. My dad makes me pay room and board, but it's a lot less than I'd have to pay for a place of my own."

Susannah winced at the words "unlike you," spoken so sharply. They hurt. Still, they were accurate. She and Sam wouldn't be paying their own college bills.

Then again, this was the first time Lily had ever talked to her about anything. She didn't want to ruin it by taking offense.

"Even when I do get there," Lily continued, hugging her arms around her chest as a sharp blast of frigid air whooshed in through the plastic flap, "I can't afford to live on campus. I'll still have to live at home and take the bus." The expression on her lovely face was bleak. "Sometimes I think I'll never get out of that house."

Then, Lily said something that surprised Susannah. "So, has your brother come back yet?"

Susannah, astonished, replied with a simple "No." Then added, "I didn't know you knew he'd left." What she really meant was, I didn't know you knew Samuel Grant III existed.

"Kate told me." Lily waved a hand toward the door. "I couldn't believe he was dumb

152

enough to go out in this. On foot yet! To find some family he doesn't even know."

Susannah was sure she heard grudging admiration in Lily's voice.

"I can't decide if that makes him really brave or really stupid," Lily added.

Susannah thought, Oh, yeah, you *have* decided. Well, well, well. Wait'll I tell Sam. When he gets back, the news that Lily Dolan was worried about him will warm him up a lot faster than hot chicken noodle soup.

Then her anxiety returned, wiping the smile off her face. *When* Sam returned? Or *if*?

chapter
18

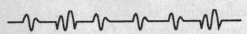

Sid came to with a start. His heart began pounding furiously as he realized that he had fallen asleep.

Idiot! He had fallen asleep in a closed car with the heater on.

This time he shouted aloud. "Jerk! What is *wrong* with you? How many times after the accident did you tell a shrink that you were *not* suicidal? Were you lying? Do you have a death wish, after all? Because sleeping in a closed car with the heater on is a great way to get that wish!"

His hand flew out to switch off the ignition.

And if there had been poisonous fumes inside the car from a blocked exhaust pipe? He'd be dead now, it was that simple. Dead. Not just paralyzed, which admittedly had its drawbacks but still left him with plans for the future, but dead, with no future at all.

"You *said* you were going to stay awake," Sid muttered furiously.

He knew he couldn't have slept more than a

few minutes. The van wasn't that hot yet. And he felt okay. Some instinct for self-preservation must have yanked him awake. Saved his life. Not that he deserved it, but he was grateful.

When he was fully alert, he rolled down the window on the driver's side, to let fresh air in and to clear the glass of snow so that he could see. Frigid air and snow poured in. He waited only a few seconds before rolling the window up.

"Lot of good that did," he complained. Although the glass was clear now, there was nothing out there but white. "I'm alone in the middle of the damn Antarctic!" Sid grumbled aloud.

It was time to do something, he knew that. He couldn't just sit like a lump and wait to die.

Sid laughed harshly. As if he could do anything *but* sit.

"Now wait a minute," he said, speaking the words loudly. "Did you or did you not get Billy Griffin down out of that tree during the refinery fire? So what do you mean, all you can do is sit? You can do better than that. Quit feeling sorry for yourself."

Reaching up, he switched on the overhead light. It was so pathetically dim, it was almost as bad as having no light at all.

Swiveling his head, Sid scrutinized the back

of the van for something that might help him. What he needed to do was make the van more noticeable, in case someone came along.

I could always set it on fire, Sid thought wryly. That'd be hard to miss.

Reality check here. Who was going to be out on a night like this? His only hope was an emergency vehicle of some kind. Ambulance. Fire truck. Police car. But even if someone did drive by, they'd never spot the van unless he did something to make it visible.

He could see nothing in the back of the van that would help. There were piles of blankets back there, which he would need if his stay out here was extended. At least he'd be warm. And there was a large white box with a red cross on the lid. Medical supplies. Might need those, too, eventually. That was all he could see from the driver's seat.

He would have to crawl back there and check things out firsthand. It was the only way. He had no idea how he'd hoist himself up over the back of the front seat and then over the backseats into the storage space in the rear of the van. Such a task seemed impossible.

But he *would* make his way to the back of the van, and he *would* find something that would be useful in calling attention to the van. He'd do whatever he had to, to stay alive until someone came along and saw him. That was the plan. And the plan would work.

Because the plan *had* to work.

Callie Matthews was bored silly. After being rushed through the "picnic" dinner spread out on her father's desk, he had shooed her out of his office, saying he had "a million things to do."

Big shock there. He always had a million things to do. What was she supposed to do with the rest of the night? She couldn't very well go home. She didn't have her car, and wouldn't have driven it in this weather anyway, not after the way it had spun out on her on the way over here.

Afraid that someone would steal or strip her beloved car, she had tried to call a towing service, but the lines had been busy.

"You left a thirty-five-thousand dollar car sitting in the middle of the street?" her father had accused. "Wasn't it operational?"

"Well, yes, of course it was. But it was giving me a hard time, Daddy. Sliding all over the road on that awful ice. And I didn't leave it in the middle of the street. I left it partly on someone's lawn. After it slid off the road, I was afraid to keep driving it. You wouldn't want me to have an accident, would you?"

She had changed the subject quickly then, anxious to tell him about the vagrants Kate Thompson had fed in the hospital's kitchen. She knew he would be as horrified and disgusted as she was.

But he wasn't. To Callie's dismay, when she'd finished telling her story, Caleb Matthews shrugged and said, "Everybody has to eat, Callie. We waste a lot of food downstairs. As a matter of fact, Samuel's been talking about getting in touch with some of the shelters in town, seeing if we can't make arrangements to share what we can't use. Some of the restaurants in town are already doing that. According to him, anyway."

Callie was stunned. She had expected, at the very least, a pat on the head for getting rid of those people. At the very most, she'd hoped that maybe as a reward, he'd leave the hospital and go home with her. The night nurse was with her mother, who'd had a really bad day, but it would be much nicer if her father came home. They could send the night nurse away, build a fire in the fireplace in her mother's bedroom, and watch a video together, the whole family. Maybe something funny, to cheer her mother up.

It didn't look like that was going to happen.

She had thought her father would be furious with Kate, maybe even decide to get rid of her. Callie didn't like Kate. She was arrogant, always walking with her head up, like a queen or something.

Her father wasn't mad at Kate, though. He didn't even care about the vagrants.

She hated it when he talked about Susannah and Sam's father, Samuel Grant. Like he worshipped the man. It was sickening. She was convinced that one of the reasons her father worked so much overtime was to impress Mr. Grant, who was on Med Center's board of directors. He *ran* the board, in fact. The man was president of practically every group or board in town.

Big deal. Her father was important, too. Didn't he run this entire, enormous, medical complex?

His lack of anger with Kate was bitterly disappointing. Callie felt very alone. If her father wasn't on her side, who *was*?

He'd dismissed her, as he always did. Now she had no clue what she was going to do with the rest of the night.

Walking sullenly along the tenth floor hallway, the heels of her boots sinking into the thick carpet, her red shoulder bag swinging on her shoulder, Callie wondered where Sam was. She'd seen him here, earlier. Gawking at that red-haired nurse's aide, the one with the drunken father. Trash, that's all Lily Dolan was, even if she was a hotshot student at Grant High last year. Lily's picture had been in the paper in June, right before graduation. Callie's mother had said, "My, isn't she lovely?"

Okay, so Lily was pretty. Gorgeous, even, but Sam couldn't possibly be thinking of asking that girl out. Could he?

If he was still around, Callie decided she'd find him and talk him into going down to the cafeteria with her. She loved flirting with Sam. He usually flirted back. And there was always the hope, which she clung to tenaciously, that one day he'd wake up and see that she was the perfect girl for him. So far, he didn't take her seriously. But then, Sam didn't take *any* girl seriously.

Someday, Samuel Grant III would be ready to settle down, and that would require just the *right* female. No one in town would be a better match for him than Callie Matthews.

So she was perfectly willing to be patient, waiting for Sam to see that. And he would.

In the meantime, tonight was the perfect opportunity to lay some more groundwork with Sam. She didn't know why he was at the hospital, unless it was because of that Dolan girl. Whatever. He wasn't a volunteer, so he wouldn't be busy like Susannah and Kate and Will and Abby. He'd have time for Callie. And later, since she didn't have her car, she'd wangle a ride home with him.

Callie was smiling all the way down in the elevator.

"Seen Sam?" she asked Susannah as they were about to pass in a hallway. Susannah was walking so fast, Callie had to step in front of her to slow her down.

"He left. But I expect him back here at any minute." Then Susannah stepped around Callie and hurried away.

He'd left? The disappointment of that piece of news was tempered by the information that wherever Sam had gone, he was on his way back. She would meet him at the door, grab him before someone else did. Someone like Lily Dolan.

Head high, blonde hair swaying on her shoulders, Callie walked confidently to the double glass doors. The only remaining evidence of that stupid accident with the ambulance was the tacky plastic stapled to the wall. Her father ought to fire that ambulance driver.

It was freezing cold by the door. Her bright red coat was warm enough, but she found herself wishing she'd worn leggings or tights under her boots. Her legs were cold. She was leaning against the wall, staring at the snowstorm outside but not really seeing it, when her car came to a stop in front of the entrance.

Callie jerked away from the wall, standing upright. She stared. *Her* car. Here. At Med Center. When she'd left it, hours earlier, on Linden Boulevard.

What was her car doing here?

Her first thought was that her father, worried about what would happen to it, had sent someone to pick it up and bring it back here for her.

Then the driver's side door opened, and Sam stepped out.

Callie's face lit up. Sam had gone after her car? If that wasn't just the sweetest thing! She hadn't even asked him to.

But . . . she hadn't given him the keys, either. How . . . ?

Of course. He knew about the extra key she kept under the car. He must have used it. What a sweetie he was, going out in this weather just for her.

Callie laughed with delight. That was some act Sam put on, pretending he didn't have strong feelings for her. But she'd known all along, hadn't she? Who was he kidding, anyway . . .

Wait a minute. Someone else was getting out of the car. A woman, small and thin, with long, dark hair, carrying a bundle in her arms.

A man left the car next, moving stiffly, as if he was in pain. A patient?

What would a patient be doing in *her* car?

Sam had turned toward the back of the car and was reaching inside to help someone climb out. A little boy with curly hair. He was quickly followed by another passenger, this one a girl, taller and skinnier than the boy. Her thin face looked sullen.

Callie realized then, with a sharp intake of her breath, who the people were. No . . . it couldn't be! That family of vagrants Kate Thompson had fed couldn't possibly have been riding in her car. No way.

Dizzy with the horror of it, Callie struggled to think clearly. She realized what must have happened. They had found her car sitting on the boulevard and tried to steal it. Sam had stopped them. Yes, of course, that's exactly what had happened. Sam had been brave enough to stop the thieves when he caught them in the act. He had probably risked his very life for *her*.

Callie thought with pleasure, I will have to buy him something really nice to thank him. What do you buy someone who already has everything?

She'd think of something.

The people seemed to be holding back. Sam

was urging them inside, out of the storm . . . Callie could see that none of them was dressed warmly enough for the weather . . . but they looked afraid. The woman was arguing with the man.

The questions that popped into Callie's mind then arrived without her permission, startling her.

Why was Sam treating these would-be thieves so kindly? Why was he smiling at them, nodding reassuringly, obviously trying in a very gentle way to urge them inside?

More important, if he really had caught these people trying to steal her car, why was he bringing them back here to Med Center when he should have been taking them straight to the police station?

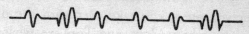

Sam was not disappointed by Callie's reaction. As he shepherded the Sloan family into the hospital, he watched her expression change from shock to relief and then to confusion. Clearly, she hadn't yet made up her mind about what to think yet.

Callie was quickly set straight when Sam finally spoke. "Kate sent me looking for these nice people. She was worried about them. I found them out in the storm and gave them a ride in your car. Hope you don't mind, Callie. Look at it this way, we did you a favor, right? Your car is here now, so you won't have to walk home." He was grinning maddeningly as he tossed her the extra key. "Man, that thing handles like a dream. I can't figure out how you let it get away from you."

Stupefied, all Callie could manage was a weak, "Sam . . . ?"

But he had already turned away from her, back to the family.

Placing a friendly arm around the five-year-old boy's shoulders, Sam said cheerfully, "Okay, folks, let's go find my sister. She's a volunteer here. She'll see to it that the little one," patting the bundle in the woman's arms, "sees a doctor right away. And Abby O'Connor, another volunteer, can take over with the other two kids while Mom and Pop see what the doc has to say, okay? O'Connor's good with kids. She's got a whole bunch of brothers and sisters at home."

Callie's mouth fell open as Sam led the five away.

She was still standing there, frozen, when Lily Dolan approached, pushing a laundry cart. "Better close your mouth, Matthews," she said, looking amused, "before someone pops a pill into it. You're in a hospital, you know."

Callie had absolutely no interest in striking up a friendship with Lily Dolan. Under normal circumstances, she wouldn't even have answered Lily. But her shock and rage were so great, she had to tell someone what had just happened to her, and there was no one else to tell.

To her chagrin, Lily brightened visibly as Callie babbled her story about the "vagrants," about Kate sending Sam out into the storm after them, and about how Sam had compounded the crime by bringing them back to the hospital in *her* car. Then she added hotly that if you asked *her*, the minute the littlest kid, who seemed to be sick, had been treated, that family should be tossed out of Emsee.

But Lily had long since stopped listening. "No kidding?" she cried when Callie finally ran out of breath. "Sam Grant? For real? I thought that was him." She smiled, a quiet, secret smile that Callie didn't understand. "Sam Grant, how about that?" Lily murmured again. Then she snapped out of it and said cheerfully, "Well, thanks, Matthews, I appreciate the info. See ya!" And off she went. She was laughing as she left Callie standing there alone.

Shaking with fury, Callie took a few deep breaths to calm herself. When she had done so, she reviewed the offenses against her. First, there was Sam. Sam hadn't discovered the family stealing her car, after all. He had actually been *looking* for them. He'd found them out in the snowstorm and brought them back to the hospital. In *her* car!

Why *her* car? Why *hadn't* he brought those people here in his van?

And then, there was Lily. Callie could have cut out her own tongue for babbling the way she had to that stupid girl. Lily had thought it was *funny*. Funny! Well, it wasn't *her* car those people had sat in. How dare she laugh at Callie Matthews?

And last, but certainly not least, the Sloans. Something had to be done about them. They had no business using the hospital as a refuge. There were shelters. Places they could go.

Maybe the youngest one *was* sick. Callie had heard a nasty cough as they passed by. She'd give them just enough time to have the kid checked out . . . no one could accuse *her* of being heartless . . . and then she was calling the proper authorities. *Somebody* had to do something to keep this hospital from turning into a shelter. People would thank her later.

Then, she was on her way to listen outside the cubicle where the child had been taken for treatment. The second she heard a doctor say, "There, I guess that'll do it!" Callie Matthews was running to the nearest telephone to dial 911 and get the police out here to cart the family away.

It wasn't easy to be sneaky in high-heeled boots that clickety-clacked on the hard white floor tile, but Callie managed.

She'd had a lot of practice.

Inside the cubicle, the Sloan parents stood by anxiously while Dr. Izbecki examined the child lying flushed and restless on the table. Sam, Susannah, and Kate stood off to one side, watching. They had already thanked Sam profusely. Abby had taken the other two children upstairs to pediatrics to borrow some books and toys.

"This child is not dressed appropriately for the weather," the doctor said sternly, keeping his stethoscope on the child's chest. It was clearly a reprimand, and both parents flushed in shame, though they said nothing in their own defense.

Lily Dolan poked her auburn head into the room. "So, how's it going?" she asked, directing her question to Sam. "I heard you went on a rescue mission." Tall and graceful, she moved on into the room to stand beside Sam. "Is she going to be okay?"

"It looks like croup," Izbecki told her. Of Mrs. Sloan, he asked, "Has she had it before?"

The woman nodded. "Once. I had to make a croup tent in her bedroom."

"I'm going to admit her," he told the baby's parents.

They exchanged a worried glance. "Ah . . ." Mr. Sloan began reluctantly, "I'm not working just now. We don't have insurance."

Izbecki waved a hand. "I said I'm admitting her. I'm the doctor, I can do that. You'll have to talk to someone else about insurance."

Kate went upstairs with the doctor, the parents, and the child. In the cubicle, Susannah turned to Lily. "Your father hasn't shown up yet, has he?"

Lily's bruised face paled noticeably. "Nope. Not yet." She glanced up at the big, round clock high on one wall. "Maybe he's already home, sleeping it off. But," she sighed, "probably not." Shaking her head, she fixed thickly lashed, dark blue eyes on Susannah and said, "I think I hear Mulgrew calling you."

Susannah tilted her head, listening. "Really? I don't . . ." She saw Lily's gaze move to Sam, and she understood. With a perfectly straight face, she said, "Oh, yeah, you're right. I hear it, too. See ya!"

Looking a bit puzzled, Sam said, "I didn't hear anyone calling her name. If I didn't know better, I'd think you were deliberately trying to get rid of Susannah."

Lily leaned against the wall. "You *don't* know better. You just think you do."

Shocked, Sam studied her, thinking he'd never seen anyone look quite so pretty in one of those uniforms. "Let me get this straight. I don't want to jump the gun here. Are you saying you wanted to be alone with me?"

Lily kept her head up, looking him directly in the eyes. "That's what I'm saying. Can you deal with it?"

Sam nodded. "Absolutely."

"I just wanted to tell you," she said clearly, "I think what you did was great. Going out in this storm to bring that family back. You didn't have to do that. It was . . . it was nice."

Nice. Even though he was still frozen to the core, and he was convinced his frostbitten fingers would never work properly again, Sam wasn't offended by the mildness of the word. Coming from Lily, it seemed like high praise. "Thanks," he said, smiling at her. "That means a lot to me."

She smiled, too. "It does? Why?"

She wasn't being coy, Sam realized. She meant it. She wanted to know why he cared what she thought. That made sense. They didn't really know each other. As far as she was concerned, there was no reason why he should be interested in what she thought or how she felt.

He had to be careful here. He didn't want to scare her off by telling her that he *was* interested, and had been for a while. Go slow, he told himself, really slow. Don't blow this one.

"It means a lot to me," he finally answered, "because I want to get to know you. Any chance you could go downstairs for a cup of coffee?"

Lily nodded. "Every chance. I haven't had a break all night." She walked over to Sam, smiling up at him. "I'm buying, though. It's your reward for a job well done. Besides," she added with a glint in her eyes, "I get an employee discount downstairs. If you paid, it would cost more."

As they left the cubicle, they didn't notice Callie Matthews lurking behind an open door a few feet down the hall. And they didn't see the look of pure hatred in her eyes.

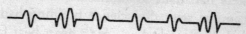

Sid had no idea how long it took him to find the lantern that just might save his life. It hadn't been easy. His shoulders were wide, and for one terrible moment, with his head and neck already through the gap and facing the backseats, he had thought he was stuck. Being found in that position would have been totally humiliating.

It was that thought that forced him to push and wiggle and squeeze until his shoulders finally popped through the gap. Then he dragged the rest of his body through until he was lying on the floor between the front and backseats.

At first, he thought he'd have to climb over them. Then he realized that the backseat didn't go all the way across. The narrow aisle near the sliding door would allow him to drag himself back to the rear of the van without hauling himself up over the seat.

The carpet was rough, and scratched his hands, elbows, and forearms as he dragged himself to the back of the van. Then he saw it. Huge and powerful — an ugly, green metal monster of a light with a wire handle. It was similar in size and shape to the lights rescue workers had used to illuminate the blast site on campus after the science building had exploded. If it worked . . . Sid's heart beat faster . . . it would light up the inside of the van like a fireworks display. If it worked . . .

It worked. He pushed the button on the lantern's left side, the batteries kicked in, and the van's interior sprang to life.

"Yes, yes, *yes!*" With this light sitting beside him on the front seat, or hanging from the rearview mirror or stashed on the dash, someone passing by couldn't fail to see the van. And him.

But the euphoria evaporated quickly. That "if" of someone passing by was a big one. It wasn't just the lateness of the hour. Sid glanced at his watch. After eleven. On an ordinary night, there *would* be people out after eleven. But on a night like this, no one in their right mind would be out.

The light helped. It helped a lot. He felt less alone, less lost. But it wasn't going to be of much use if no one saw it.

Too exhausted to repeat his journey to the front of the van, Sid peeled one of the blankets off the pile, wrapped it around him, and sank back against a folded wheelchair. Its brake poked him uncomfortably between his shoulder blades, but he was too tired to shift position again.

He closed his eyes.

"We have to go look for him," Abby pleaded with Damon. "Sid's been out there for hours now. No one's seen him, or heard from him. There's no phone in his van, so he can't call for help. Please, Damon. Kate said you're off-duty now. I'll come with you, okay? But we have to go *now*!"

Damon had come into the ER to be treated for mild smoke inhalation following a house fire involving a faulty space heater. He was fine, and wanted to return to his fire truck, but his captain had said no way, and taken him off the roster.

Kate had stayed with him the whole time he was being given oxygen in a treatment room. But he could tell by the look in her eyes that she was anxious to return to the Sloan baby upstairs, so after just one quick but satisfying kiss, he'd told her to go.

Abby had stopped him on his way out of the treatment room. "I don't know who else to ask, Damon. I've tried a dozen times to call the police, but the line is always busy. I suppose they're going nuts, too. And Sam was already out there so long, finding the Sloans, I can't ask him. Will's still on ambulance duty. I think he's planning to stay on all night. That leaves you, Damon. Anyway, you've been trained in rescue techniques, right? In case . . . in case Sid is hurt or something."

Damon didn't ask what the "or something" might mean.

He knew Abby had every reason to worry. Costello had come a long way since last summer when he'd fallen from the water tower. Damon saw him out and about a lot now, navigating his wheelchair around town, eating in restaurants with friends, parked in an aisle at a movie theater, even spinning his chair around a dance floor with O'Connor sitting on his lap. It took guts to do that. Sid had guts, no question. But he'd need a lot more than guts if he was stranded out there.

"You got any idea where to look for him?" he asked Abby. If they were going to leave Med Center, he wished Kate would come along. He'd hardly spent two minutes with her all night. But she wouldn't want to leave until that Sloan kid was out of the woods. "He was on a home visit, right? You know where he lives?"

Abby nodded. "Yes. Just outside of town, right before you get to the cutoff to Violet's

Corners. But he could be anywhere between there and here."

"Rehab's vans are white," Damon pointed out. "If Sid skidded off the road, we'll never spot him."

"Yes, we *will*!" Abby cried, She hated pessimism at any time, but especially when it involved Sid. "Wait'll I tell Astrid we're going, then we'll leave, okay?"

"You got wheels? 'Cause the tires on my old pickup are balder than my old man."

Abby held up a set of keys. A miniature football dangled from the ring. "I borrowed Sam's van. It's heavy. It won't slide around. And the tires are good." Clutching the sleeve of Damon's red sweater, she led him toward the nurses' desk. "When I told Sam where we were going, he wanted to come with us, but I wouldn't let him. He's having coffee in the cafeteria with Lily, and when he lifted his cup, I could see that his hands were shaking a little. I knew it wasn't because of Lily. Sam Grant has never in his life been nervous around a girl. He just hasn't warmed up yet, that's all. So I told him to stay here."

"Lily Dolan and Sam? You're putting me on, right?"

"Nope." Abby shrugged. "You know Sam. He wants whatever he thinks he can't have.

Lily's never even looked his way, as far as I know, so of course she's his newest challenge. It won't last. It never does with Sam."

Damon looked at her quizzically. "Sour grapes?"

Abby laughed. "Get real. I like Sam okay. But he's my best friend's brother, so I know more about him than most people. He is absolutely, positively not my type. I want someone who actually believes I am the only perfect person in the world for him. Sid believes that. I can't imagine Sam Grant believing that of any girl. But," shrugging, "maybe one day. Who knows? It could even be Lily, I suppose . . . except that both of Sam's parents would have a stroke if he ever brought Tommy Dolan's daughter to dinner."

Astrid wasn't at the desk, so Abby jotted a quick note on the head nurse's blotter. Then she darted into the lounge to grab her coat, scarf, and gloves, and left the ER with Damon.

When they passed the plastic sheets stapled over the huge, gaping hole, she said, "You must have been petrified when you found out Kate was underneath that ambulance, right? I know *I* was. It was probably worse for you."

When Damon nodded grimly, Abby thought with conviction, That's why he's taking me to look for Sid. Because he remembers how awful it felt, thinking Kate was hurt, or worse.

She had thought she wanted Sam or Will to go with her, because she knew them better. But as they climbed into Sam's silver van in the parking garage, she decided that Damon was exactly the right person. He knew how she felt. He'd try as hard as he could to find Sid.

They were nearly broadsided on their way out of the complex by a huge old station wagon skidding and sliding crazily from one side of the wide, tree-lined driveway to the other. It narrowly missed the van as it flew by.

"Must have bad tires," Abby commented, heaving a sigh of relief as the careening car raced off, toward Grant Memorial.

"I don't *think* so," Damon said, steering the van expertly out onto the highway. "The driveway isn't that slippery. Been a whole lot of traffic on it tonight and it's packed the snow down over the ice. You ask me, that dude's been pouring a few down his throat."

"You think he was drunk?"

"Better believe it. Now, which way do we turn here?"

"Left."

Behind them, the rusty old station wagon screeched to a halt in the ER's driveway. The door opened, and a man in a plaid wool jacket, his head bare, pulled himself out by holding onto the door handle. He stood unsteadily in the blowing snow for a few minutes, then slammed the door shut and began weaving his way toward the entrance, muttering under his breath.

What he was muttering, had anyone been around to hear, sounded suspiciously like, "Show her, I'll show her, got no respect, no respect at all, I'll show her."

chapter
21

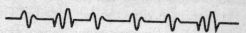

Other ambulances continued to arrive fast and furiously. In spite of the pace, patients were handled, as always, with speed and great care. Most of them were too sick or injured upon arrival to notice that one wall of the emergency entrance looked very odd indeed, with wildly flapping plastic where there should have been solid brick.

Susannah didn't know the paramedics who came hurrying in with a patient whose neck had been immobilized by a collar and sandbags. She knew only that the three men were friends of Will's, and could see that he hadn't been on this particular run. She hadn't seen him in a while.

Kate had just come back downstairs. She told Susannah the Sloan baby was "holding her own," and that Kate had spent the last half an hour trying to locate a social worker. They'd all gone home early because of the storm, and she'd had to try reaching them by phone. So far, she hadn't had any luck.

"Telephone lineman," the taller man in snow-whitened navy blue said cryptically. "He fell from the top of a pole and landed on an icy spot the wind had swept free of snow. No nice, soft, snow-pillow for this guy." Addressing Dr. Santiago directly, he added, "Thirty-four-year-old male, conscious, open fracture left femur. Patient oriented, no neck pain, pupils equal and reactive."

Susannah noticed the traction splint sticking out from beneath the blanket covering the patient. An open fracture was tricky. Pushing the exposed bone ends back into the site of the wound in order to splint the limb could mean an infection later. But in many cases like this one, the paramedics decided on the spot that since the patient would require surgery to repair the break, any necessary cleaning of the wound could be done at the same time. Antibiotics, if necessary, could be given at the hospital to offset any possible damage done by the bone ends reentering the wound. More often than not, the paramedics went ahead and splinted at the scene, which made the patient a little more comfortable during the trip to the hospital.

"Pulse ninety-two, respirations eighteen, blood pressure one-eighteen over seventy," the paramedic called out as the pneumatic doors hissed closed behind them. "No dorsalis pedis pulse. But he's complaining of pain, so no loss of sensation in the limb yet."

Susannah and Kate knew that was a good sign. The man must have fallen a long way from the top of the utility pole. He could have suffered a serious spinal injury, as Sid had when he fell. But though there was no pulse in the foot, the fact that the man could still feel the limb probably ruled out a spinal cord injury. Maybe he'd been lucky.

The doors had barely closed behind the gurney when another ambulance arrived.

"You two go back out there," Astrid called over her shoulder, indicating Susannah and Kate with a wave of her hand. "See what's up. We'll take care of this one. Dr. Lincoln will be there in a minute."

This time, it was Will who jumped from the rear of the ambulance. Susannah could tell by the expression in his dark eyes that there'd be no rushing with this patient. It was too late. Dr. Lincoln, just now pushing her way through the doors, would have to write DOA . . . their first of the night . . . on the chart. Dead on Arrival. No need to hurry, not this time.

I'll never get used to it, Susannah vowed, watching as Will and one of his partners eased the gurney from the back of the vehicle as gently and carefully as they would have if the patient were still alive. They had already covered the victim's face.

"Whose station wagon is that?" Will asked irritably. "It's not supposed to be parked this close to the ambulance entrance."

Susannah turned to look. The car was old, rusted, and parked at an odd angle, as if the driver had left it in a hurry. There was just enough room left in the driveway for an ambulance to pass. "Maybe someone had an emergency," she offered, although she didn't remember anyone coming in alone in the past hour or so. But then, it was hard to keep all of the emergencies straight, there'd been so many.

A second vehicle, this one an old Ford pick-up truck, skidded up the driveway, narrowly missing the parked car before stopping abruptly behind the ambulance. The truck wasn't in much better shape than the station wagon.

Two people jumped free, a tall, heavyset man in a plaid flannel shirt and jeans under a wrinkled denim jacket, and a short, plump woman in red sweatpants and a fat, red down jacket.

The man had been crying, but the woman was dry-eyed, and clearly angry. Neither walked too steadily, but as they approached Susannah, she smelled no liquor.

"I *told* him," the woman shouted as they

reached the paramedics entering the hospital with the covered gurney, "to get that damn furnace checked before winter set in. I *told* him! But oh, no, he wasn't about to spend the money. My husband the tightwad! Now look, just look!" She pointed with one plump finger toward the gurney. "His own father, the sweetest old man in the world, dead before his time, from that stupid furnace!"

Dr. Lincoln took the relatives of the dead man into a cubicle, while Will explained to Susannah and Kate, "That woman was right about the furnace. It was leaking fumes. The grandfather, the guy who died, was asleep in a bedroom upstairs, right over the furnace room. The living room, where everyone else was watching television, was at the other end of the house. When the woman went upstairs to check on the old guy, like she did every night, it was too late. Then these two started feeling sick, too. They knew enough to get out of the house right away and go to a neighbor's to call 911. They weren't exposed long, but it looks like they've got some damage. That's probably why the woman was going on and on like she was. They'll need oxygen to clear their heads."

After suggesting that they get security to check the station wagon, Will went on into the treatment cubicle to fill out his report on the relatives of the dead man.

Kate went back upstairs, and Susannah went into the waiting room to ask if anyone owned a beige station wagon.

No one did.

She went next to the security office to report the illegally parked car. Then she tagged along as one of the guards went outside to check the station wagon for proof of ownership. She watched from inside as he opened the door, fumbled around in the glove compartment, and dug out a piece of paper. When he had read it, he replaced it, left the car, and closed the door. His expression was glum.

"*What?*" Susannah asked when he came inside, stamping snow off his boots. "What's wrong?"

"We got trouble," he said heavily, glancing suspiciously around the lobby area. "That car belongs to Tommy Dolan."

"Oh, no," Susannah breathed, thinking of Lily.

"He been admitted here tonight as a patient?"

Susannah shook her head. "No." She would have heard if Lily's father had been brought in. Even if no one had told her, Tommy Dolan never came into the ER quietly.

"Then he drove himself. And not very well, judging by the way that car is parked. He's gotta have a snootful, like always. I wonder where he is?"

"Probably looking for his daughter," Susannah said emphatically. "And she's in the cafeteria with my brother." She was already walking toward the stairs. "You'd better come with me," she called over her shoulder, "because if Lily is right, her father came here to pick a fight."

"So what else is new?" the security guard replied. But he was right behind her.

The cafeteria was crowded. There was an air of fatigue about the place reflected in the dim lighting, the stale doughnuts in their plastic case, the coffee thickening to a mudlike consistency in glass pots. Faces were pale and strained, eyes red-rimmed.

Lily Dolan and Sam Grant were the exception. Sitting at a small side table against the far wall, they sipped coffee and talked as if it were an ordinary night. There was not the slightest sign of fatigue in either of them.

Sam had gradually warmed up, his hands steady now as he lifted a doughnut to his mouth. "Grant U? I wouldn't mind. It's a good school. But my dad has his heart set on me going to an Ivy League school. Susannah hasn't given up yet. She still says she's staying in Grant, going to college here, with Kate and

Abby and Will. I hear that friend of Kate's, Damon Lawrence is going there, too. My dad's giving Susannah a hard time about it, but . . ."

Lily smiled. "I've watched your sister work. If she really wants to go to Grant U, I'll bet she does."

Disappointed that she hadn't said the same thing about him, but telling himself it was only because she didn't know him as well as she did Susannah, Sam simply nodded. Then, even though he was afraid of pushing her away and knew that what he was about to say might do just that, he had to say it. "You shouldn't let someone hit you." His voice was quiet, but firm.

Lily's face flushed, and her eyes went cold. "You don't know anything about it," she said flatly. She wasn't looking at him now, but focusing her eyes on the salt and pepper shakers on the table. "He wasn't always like this. When I was little, I got so excited when I knew it was time for him to come home from work. He was so much fun."

"What happened?"

Lily sighed. But she didn't look at him. "I had a little brother. The son my dad always wanted. I was five when he was born. He died when he was four. Leukemia. They brought him here, and the doctors did everything they could. Andy put up a really good fight, but it wasn't enough. After that, well, things just sort of went downhill. My dad started drinking, and he never stopped."

"I'm sorry," was all Sam could think of to say. "That's rough."

"He hates this place now. One of the worst fights we ever had was when I took this job. We've been fighting about it ever since. I know it wasn't the doctors' fault, and so does my mom. But my dad just never got over it. It was like he had to have someone to blame, and Med Center was it."

"Are you going into medicine then, like Susannah?"

Lily did look up, then. She shook her head. "No. I want to teach. First or second grade." Her face eased then, and she laughed lightly. "I want to get my hands on them early."

"Going to change the world?" Sam asked, smiling. An impossible task, of course. But watching Lily, seeing the determination in her lovely face and hearing it in her voice, he knew that she was going to give it her best shot.

"Maybe," she said, returning his smile.

She was *not* just another pretty face, and Sam was ashamed that he'd ever thought that of her.

He was about to ask her out to dinner Saturday night when a deep, slurred voice bellowed from the doorway on the opposite side of the room, "There you are, Miss High-and-Mighty!"

Lily gasped, and Sam's head shot up. Their eyes flew to the doorway.

Tommy Dolan, all six feet, two hundred and sixty pounds of him, stood there, weaving slightly, his beefy face flushed red with cold and alcohol, his narrowed eyes fixed on his daughter. "An' look who she's sittin' with: The richest brat in town." His booming voice shook the glasses sitting on the counter. They made a faint tinkling sound. "No wonder she got herself a job here. I figured she was fixin' to catch herself a rich doctor." He laughed bitterly, an evil sound. "Turns out, she had her eyes on the prize the whole time. Samuel Grant's son hisself!"

Lily's face was scarlet. She sat frozen, unable to move.

Tommy Dolan's broad, ruddy face spread into a nasty leer. "Like we don't know what the Grant son and heir wants from my little girl, right, folks? *She* may be too dumb to figure it out, but her old man ain't. No one puts anything over on Tommy Dolan."

As everyone in the room stared in disgust, Lily's father left the doorway and began lurching unsteadily across the room.

He was headed straight for Lily and Sam's table.

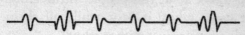

"I'll handle this," Lily said under her breath as she and Sam stood up. "Stay out of it."

All eyes in the cafeteria were on them. Tommy Dolan had shut up, as if he couldn't concentrate on weaving his way among the chairs and tables and talk at the same time. The only sound in the room was the hissing of steam in the pipes and the distant clanking of dishes in the kitchen area.

Head high, chin thrust forward defiantly, Lily waited for her father. Tall and slim in her pale blue pantsuit, red hair slipping loose of its rubber band, she looked like a warrior prepared to do battle.

When Tommy Dolan, red-faced and breathing hard, arrived at the table, Lily took the offensive. "What are you doing here?" she inquired. She kept her voice low. It was cold and flat. "I'm working."

He laughed. "Oh, I can see that, missy." He nodded vigorously, thick, graying hair falling across his forehead. "Workin', right. I can see that you're just toilin' away here in this death trap." He glanced around the room with narrow, hate-filled eyes. Raising his voice again, he shouted, "No wonder people die in this place! Look at all you people, sittin' around on your cans, takin' it easy, while all them sick people upstairs just wither away!"

"Don't talk to them like that!" Lily ordered sharply. "They've been doing double-duty since the storm started. They're exhausted. Get out of here. No one wants you around. Go home and sleep it off."

Sam felt foolish and helpless, standing by while Lily and her father faced off. But she had asked him to butt out, and he wanted to respect that. He had to admit, so far she was holding her own.

"Don't tell me what to do, girl," Dolan warned. "I'll go, but you're coming with me. I want you out of this place, now!"

A dish dropped in the kitchen, shattering when it hit the tile. The sound rang out in the silent room like a clang of cymbals. Everyone in the room except the three at the table jumped.

"I'm not going anywhere. I told you, I'm working," Lily said, turning to leave.

Dolan's face twisted in rage. In a sudden motion surprisingly swift for someone so inebriated, his right arm flew backward, preparing to swing forward and deliver a forceful blow against the pretty head that had insulted him by turning away.

Someone in the room gasped, and Lily looked up.

The arm swung.

Sam caught it in an iron grip between wrist and elbow, when it was just inches from Lily's right ear.

Maintaining his grip, he pushed his face close to Dolan's. "You. Don't. Want. To. Do. That." Sam's gaze never wavered from the man's eyes.

Realizing what had almost happened, Lily watched, holding her breath, her eyes wide.

Although Sam's tone was more relaxed when he spoke again, his grip was not. "If you touch one hair on that girl's head, you are going straight to prison, you got that?"

Dolan's upper lip curled in scorn, but it didn't match the look in his eyes, which were pale with fear. He tried, but failed, to put a measure of contempt in his words. "You think you scare me, rich kid?"

"I want you to leave *now*," Sam said in that same easy, level voice. "You will turn around and walk out of this room, and you won't look back."

When Sam let go, the man's face crumpled. All pretense at defiance gone, he appealed to his daughter. "Aw, Lil, you know I didn't mean nothin'. How about if you come on home with me now, and we'll talk all this over, how does that sound?"

"It sounds like garbage," Lily responded unforgivingly. "The minute I get in that car with you, you'll start smacking me around. Forget it. I'm not talking about anything with you until you're stone-cold sober. Do what Sam said, Dad. Go home."

The man turned reluctantly, took a few steps, turned his head to ask plaintively, "You comin' home tonight, Lil?"

"No. Maybe I won't come home at all."

"Aww . . . " His head hung. He was a pathetic sight.

Sighing, Lily relented. "I'll call tomorrow. Just go home, Dad. Please."

When, with his head down, and his shoulders slumped, Tommy Dolan had disappeared from sight, a round of applause for Sam's bravery swept the cafeteria.

But Lily wasn't smiling up at him, her eyes shining, the way Sam had anticipated. There was anger in her face. "I told you not to interfere," she said heatedly.

Disappointed and irritated, Sam protested,

"If you expected me to stand by and let him hit you, you don't know me very well."

"No," she said, "I don't. And if you can't trust me to take care of myself, I don't think I want to know you very well." She picked up her wallet and spun away from him.

For just one tiny second, Sam felt a pang of sympathy for Tommy Dolan. Turning away from someone so coldly was cruel. It made you feel as if you didn't matter at all. The difference was, it never would have occurred to Sam to hit Lily.

She turned back to him then, and her face had changed. The anger was gone, and there were tears trembling on her lashes. "Oh, God, what's wrong with me?" she whispered. "I'm acting just like *him*. You defended me, going up against him, something hardly anyone else ever does, including my mother, and look how I thank you! By being as nasty as my father." She shook her head, then lowered it. "I'm sorry, I'm so sorry. You must hate me."

"No way." Sam was confused by her sudden shift in attitude, but he was too grateful to analyze it. What he wanted now was for that guilty, confused look on her face to disappear. "And you're not anything like him, by the way. He needs a shave, and you don't."

It worked. She was laughing when she

raised her head. "Oh, Sam," she said softly, extending one hand, "I really am sorry. Thank you."

He took the hand, closing his own around it. "Any time," he said bravely.

She laughed again. "You don't really mean that. You couldn't."

Sam wasn't sure. Maybe he *did* mean it. Gruesome as the thought of constantly going head-to-head with Tommy Dolan was, if that was what it took to keep Lily from getting hurt, maybe he could do it. "*Are* you going to go back home?" he asked as they walked, hand in hand, from the cafeteria.

"I don't know. When he sobers up, he's going to remember this and he's going to be really furious. Not only am I still working in the hospital he hates, but the person who came to my aid was Samuel Grant's son. Daddy hates your father, too. Right after Andy died, my father tied one on and burst in on a Med Center board of directors meeting. I think your dad probably felt sorry for him at first, but then my dad just wouldn't leave. So your father had him arrested. The cops didn't put him in jail that first time. They just brought him home, ranting and raving about your father. He never forgave him."

Sam groaned. "Great. Just great. So, if you do go back home, does that mean you and I are history? Before we even *have* a history?"

She answered so quickly, he knew she'd been thinking about it. "No. That's not what it means. If my father could order me around, I wouldn't be working here, would I? But Sam," she added quickly, "I don't have a lot of free time." She stopped walking, leaned against a wall in the corridor, facing him. "And I'm not a party person like you. When I have time off, which isn't very often, I like to walk along the riverbank, maybe take a book with me, and find a quiet spot to read. I jog, and I like to listen to music." Her eyes met his. "I'm pretty boring."

Sam laughed. "You? Boring?"

"I mean it," she said weakly.

He sobered then, saying seriously, "Can we just try it? Give it a shot? If it doesn't work, okay, I'll live with that." He grinned. "Look at it this way. Can you think of a better way to get even with your dad for hitting you? Dating me has to be the best possible revenge."

Lily adopted a look of feigned innocence. "Why, Sam Grant! I would never be that cold and calculating. You're talking petty revenge here, on my own father! Shame on you."

His grin widened. "So, what time should I pick you up tomorrow night?"

"Eight o'clock, on the dot. But not at my

house," she added hastily. "Pick me up here. Let's not go crazy, the first time out."

Satisfied with that, Sam walked her back to the nurses' station. Then he went looking for Susannah, to tell her the surprising news. Although he wasn't all that positive she'd be surprised. Susannah had an uncanny way of knowing things about him. Maybe because they were twins.

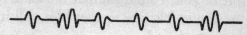

The storm raged on.

"Are you sure you're feeling okay?" Abby asked Damon. He'd been doing a fantastic job of keeping the van on the road in spite of the billowing snow, the wind battering the van, and snowdrifts the size of large shrubbery on the road. "You must have swallowed a lot of smoke in that last fire, or you wouldn't have needed oxygen. Maybe I shouldn't have asked you to do this."

Damon shook his head. "Don't worry about it. I'm cool. You're keepin' a lookout, right? Anything on that side of the road?"

"No. Not yet." It was warm inside the van, and Abby prayed with all her heart that wherever Sid was, he was warm, too. But how could he be, out in this? "Do we know where we are?"

"Yup. We're on that back road just past the cutoff to Violet's Corners."

Abby frowned. "Back road? Sid wouldn't be on a back road!"

"Yeah, he would. 'Cause if he'd been on the main one, we would have seen him. And we didn't. I figure, he took a wrong turn somewhere, easy to do when you can't see two feet in front of you. Found himself on some road with no traffic. No one to spot him, call it in, get him outa there."

It made sense.

Abby, her gloved hands clenched together in anxiety, kept her face pressed up against the window glass, scrutinizing every inch of the landscape as Damon drove slowly along the road. She could see nothing but white.

The back wheels slid, and her stomach lurched sickeningly. "Oh, God," she breathed, "please don't put us in a ditch! We'd never find Sid."

"Abby," Damon said then, "we're running low on gas. It looks like Sam forgot to fill up his tank. We can't stay out here much longer."

His voice was so kind that Abby realized exactly why Kate was in love with him, whether or not Kate admitted it. Damon had delivered the bad news about the gas tank in a voice so gentle, it had cushioned the blow, just a little. It was a voice intended to keep her from feeling too much pain. Damon Lawrence wasn't nearly as tough on the inside as he seemed to be on the outside.

Tears filled Abby's eyes. "We can't go back,"

she whispered, "we can't go back until we find him. What if he's hurt? What if he's trapped somewhere? No one else is looking for him, Damon, only us. We're all he's got. Please, please, we have to keep . . ."

She saw it then, ahead of them, off the road, a glow so distant and vaporous, she couldn't even be sure it was real. "Look, look!" she screamed. "Up there! Isn't that a light?"

Damon peered through the windshield, shook his head. "I can't tell. It could be a house, I guess."

"No, no, it's not a house, it can't be a house! Hurry, hurry!"

"Abby, Sid wouldn't have his lights on. He's been out here a while now. Even if that was him, his battery'd be dead by now. No lights." But Damon kept driving, so slowly and carefully, Abby felt like she was going to lose her mind.

It has to be Sid, she told herself over and over again as they crawled closer to the glow, it has to be, it has to be . . .

The glow grew increasingly brighter as they approached along the deserted road. Still, even when they reached a spot opposite the luminescent yellow shining out of the thick, swirling white drapery, they weren't able to identify the bulky shape on the other side of the ditch. It could have been anything . . . a

201

small shack, an abandoned bus or station wagon, a stack of logs. Except, a stack of logs wouldn't be glowing with light.

They climbed out of their own vehicle and began struggling through the drifts. The thick, persistent snowfall blinded them. Abby fell twice, landing on her chest the first time, on her side the second time. Damon helped her up, urging her on.

When they fell against the vehicle bright with the stunning yellow light, Abby cried out in triumph. "This is it! It's one of the Rehab vans, I know it is!" She began frantically to brush snow from the side facing them, until she had uncovered the letters M . . . E . . . D . . .

"See?" she shouted above the wind, "see? It's one of ours. Sid has to be here! Come on, Damon, help me get him out!"

Afraid of what she might find inside, Damon insisted on going first.

The driver's door was blocked with a snowdrift that reached Damon's shoulders. While he worked at clearing it away, Abby began shouting Sid's name at the top of her lungs, banging repeatedly on the side of the van.

There was no response from inside.

Damon said nothing, but he was worried. Okay, it was a Rehab van, Abby was right about that, and since Sid was the only person out in one that night, this had to be his. But

. . . if he *was* in there, he wasn't answering. Wouldn't he have been waiting anxiously for rescue? Maybe parked by a window, staring out at the road for the first sign of someone driving by? There was no face in any of the van's windows, peeking out and smiling because help had arrived. Why not?

Damon continued to sweep snow aside furiously. That light inside . . . that was no normal overhead light. It had to be one of those high-powered lantern things, the kind they'd used at the blast site. Sid had to have found it and turned it on. Smart move. But where was he now?

"Check around," Damon told an impatient Abby. "See if the tailpipe's exposed, okay?"

"What? What for?"

"Just *do* it, okay? Hurry up!" He didn't like what he was thinking. But they'd had a case earlier this winter . . . during another storm, not as bad as this one. Some old guy and his wife had gotten stuck in a drift, didn't know their tailpipe was buried in snow, and turned the heater on to keep from freezing to death. They hadn't frozen to death. They'd died from the fumes.

The van's engine wasn't on now, but that didn't mean anything. If Sid had turned it on to keep warm, if the fumes had backed up, he'd have . . . fallen asleep. . . . The engine would have kept going until it ran out of gas. And stopped. But by then, it could have been too late for Sid.

Still, Damon refused to give up. Even if he was right about all of this, Sid could still be alive. If it wasn't too late, he could be resuscitated.

Wishing he had resuscitation equipment with him, Damon pushed aside the last of the snow blocking the door, and reached for the handle.

"You were right," Abby said, coming around from the back of the van. "The tailpipe is completely buried. Why did you want to know?"

Damon groaned silently. Oh, God. He couldn't let her inside. Not yet. Not until . . . But how the hell was he going to keep her out? She was practically jumping out of her skin.

"Wait here," he ordered, knowing he was wasting his breath. "I'll see if he's inside."

"Of course he's inside," Abby shouted. "Where else would he be? He couldn't use his chair in *this*! Wait for me, Damon!" She still had to negotiate the distance from the rear of the van to the driver's door, through waist-high drifts.

That gave Damon the time he needed. He pulled himself up into the driver's seat. The harsh yellow light was blinding until his eyes got used to it.

Sid wasn't in the front seat. Must have stayed in the back after he'd found the lantern.

"Sid? Costello? Where the hell are you?"

"Damon?" Abby said as she struggled up into the driver's seat after him. "Where is he?"

Damon saw Sid then. In the back, wrapped to the chin in gray wool blankets, resting against a folded wheelchair leaning against one wall. His head was down, his eyes closed.

"Wait *there*!" he ordered Abby sharply as he began to make his way to the rear of the van. She knew he meant it. She waited.

When Damon reached the gray wool bundle, he crouched beside it. "Costello?" He put a hand on one shoulder. Shook gently. "Sid?" He felt for a pulse. It was there, and it was steady. His knees went weak with relief. Sid was alive.

Damon shook his shoulder again, called his name.

Sid roused slowly. He lifted his head, his eyes still closed. He opened them reluctantly. "What?" he said, his voice husky with sleep. "What's happenin'?"

Damon laughed. "You're okay, man, you're okay. O'Connor, c'mere! There's someone back here who wants to see you."

She was there in seconds, scrambling over

205

the seat and throwing herself at Sid, crying out his name joyfully. Clasping her arms around his neck, she held on as if she would never let go.

"We gotta get him outa here," Damon said. "You can do that stuff later."

Abby stripped off a glove, touched Sid's cheek. "You're so cold," she said, tears in her eyes.

His lips were numb. But he managed, "Must be the weather."

Damon grinned. He had no idea how they were going to get Sid out of the van, across the ditch and the drifts and into Sam's car. But they'd do it.

They did. Damon and Abby had to carry Sid between the two of them. It took much longer than any of them were happy with, and by the time they reached the silver van, they were all snow-covered, chilled to the bone, and exhausted.

But once inside, they were safe.

Shivering violently, Sid sat, still wrapped in his blankets now damp with snow, between the two in the front seat. As Damon found a spot where it seemed safe to turn the van around and head back to Med Center, Sid asked, "What were you two doing out here?"

Abby smiled. Sid was frozen through and probably suffering from exposure, maybe even hypothermia. But he was *alive*. He was alive and breathing and talking and sitting here beside her, and he was *going* to be all right.

Sliding as close to him as possible, she placed an arm across his shoulders and said, "We just thought it was a really nice night for a drive in the country."

His laughter then, loud and long, warmed her own frozen body.

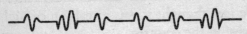

They were gathered in the Sloan baby's room. The parents stood on either side of Joanie's bed, each holding one of the child's hands underneath the croup tent. Annie was perched on the foot of the bed, eating a candy bar, and five-year-old Paulie sat on the floor, playing with half a dozen plastic cars and trucks. Susannah and Kate, on a much-needed break during a lull in the ER, stood against the wall just inside the door. Lily Dolan was adjusting the patient's IV, and Sam was sitting on a straight-backed, wooden chair, watching Lily.

"I know they're not supposed to be in here," Mrs. Sloan said, nodding toward the two younger children. "But they insist they're not going back to pediatrics until your friend, the O'Connor girl, returns. They won't talk to anyone else."

Susannah nodded. "Abby has that effect on everyone. She should be back soon. A friend of hers . . . a boy from Rehab . . . is missing."

"I hope they find him," Mr. Sloan said sincerely.

"Abby will find him," Kate said emphatically. "Bet on it."

"We're gonna spend the night at her house," Annie said happily. "She said so."

Mrs. Sloan explained. "They can't stay in pediatrics because they're not patients. Your friend Abby said her younger brother and sisters would love to have company, and since Jake and I want to stay here tonight with Joanie, we said it would be okay. The doctor said the O'Connors are lovely people, and he would vouch for them."

"Me, too," Susannah said. "And they do like a houseful of people."

Annie launched into a tale then of the wondrous toys in the pediatrics playroom. While Annie had her parents' attention, Kate spoke to Susannah in a low voice.

"I finally got in touch with a social worker," she said. "She doesn't have anything for them, not tonight. She said everything in town is crammed full. But tomorrow morning, they can move into a place on West Thirty-eighth Street." She took a small piece of paper from a pocket of her dashiki and unfolded it. "Twenty-six fifty-three West Thirty-eighth Street. She said it's not much, but it's four walls and a roof. Once they're in there, we can work on finding them something better, right?"

Susannah nodded. "And we will. I'll talk to my parents." The minute she said it, she was afraid that Kate would take offense, thinking Susannah was throwing her weight around.

On the contrary, Kate nodded and added, "Maybe your dad can find Mr. Sloan a job. That's what he really needs."

Jonah Izbecki came in then. He raised an eyebrow when he saw the crowd gathered in the room. But he said nothing. Nodding curtly toward the parents, he went straight to Joanie's bed and lifted a flap of the croup tent to listen to her chest.

Susannah wondered how many other doctors would have admitted the child without proof of insurance. Some might have given instructions for setting up a croup tent at home and sent the family on their way. Dr. Izbecki knew there was no home to go to. So he had made sure Joanie got the care she needed, and at the same time saw to it that the family had a hospital room in which to spend the night.

Susannah wasn't surprised. She'd seen enough of Dr. Izbecki's kindness to know that it was very subtle. Most people never even saw his acts of generosity, and she suspected that was exactly the way he wanted it.

"She sounds better," he said with satisfaction as he straightened up. "A good night's sleep, and she should be good as new. I heard the storm is on its way out of town. That's good news, right? A week from now, we'll be complaining that it's too warm."

"*There* they are!" a thin, high voice declared triumphantly.

All heads turned to the doorway.

Callie Matthews, flanked on both sides by uniformed policemen, was standing there, pointing one long, slender finger toward the Sloans. "I *told* you, didn't I? I told you they were hiding in here." She marched into the room and stood directly in front of Mr. Sloan. "That was a thirty-five-thousand dollar car you stole, mister, and you're not going to get away with it."

chapter

25

Mr. Sloan was the first to speak in response to Callie's shocking accusation. "You think we stole your car?"

"I *know* you stole it! I was standing right there by the door when you drove up in it. Officers, arrest this man."

Kate stiffened. Her eyes narrowed. "Get out of here and leave these people alone. You can see they have a sick child, can't you?"

Frustrated, Callie burst out angrily, "I'll bet that kid isn't even sick! This is all a plot to keep these people in the hospital when they should be in jail." Her eyes swept the room. "You're *all* in on it, every single one of you!"

Sam stood up then, moved forward easily to address the officers. "I'm the one who drove the car here," he said with a charming smile. "I'm Sam Grant."

The officers exchanged a glance.

Susannah thought, Well, being a Grant does come in handy sometimes. Like right now. If Sam really *had* stolen the car, would the police arrest him on the spot? Probably not. They'd just put in a phone call to Samuel Grant II.

Sam continued, "I and these nice people here," indicating Mr. and Mrs. Sloan, "found Callie's car stranded on Linden Boulevard. We figured the snowplow would bury it when it came along, so we rescued it. We brought it right here for Callie. Door-to-door service."

"She doesn't seem very grateful," one of the officers said, glancing at Callie, whose face was scarlet with fury.

"No, she doesn't, does she?" Sam agreed. He smiled tolerantly at Callie.

"Ask them what they were doing out on Linden Boulevard in the first place," Callie demanded of the policemen. "They were out there because they didn't have anywhere else to go. They're *vagrants*!" She spat out the last word with revulsion, the way some people might have said "serial killers."

The shorter policeman looked interested. "Vagrants?" He took a small notebook from a jacket, and moved into the room toward Mr. Sloan. "Mayor's cracking down on vagrancy," he said. "He says we gotta think about tourists. They don't like seeing people hangin' around on the streets. It gives Grant a bad name." Pencil poised over the notebook, he asked, "You just give me your home address, sir, we can clear this up right now."

Mr. Sloan's thin face paled.

"This is ridiculous," Dr. Izbecki protested angrily. "I want everyone out of this room, right *now*! This child is very ill."

No one moved. Silence fell. In the doorway, Callie looked smug. And expectant.

Watching her, Susannah thought, She can't wait for Mr. Sloan to say, "I don't have a home address." She's practically salivating.

"Well?" the policeman prodded. "Home address, please?"

Susannah and Kate looked at each other. Susannah nodded, meaning, You did all the work, so you do the honors.

Kate said clearly, "Twenty-six fifty-three West Thirty-eighth Street."

Callie frowned.

Mr. and Mrs. Sloan stared at Kate.

Dr. Izbecki smiled. So did Sam and Lily.

The policeman looked up, turned to Kate. "Excuse me?"

"Their home address is twenty-six fifth-three West Thirty-eighth Street." Kate moved forward, toward the bed. When she reached Mr. Sloan, she surreptitiously handed him the small slip of paper with his new address on it. The policeman missed the maneuver, but Sloan, guessing what it was, took it without so much as the flicker of an eyelash, and pocketed it.

"Mr. and Mrs. Sloan here," Kate told the officer smoothly, "are so concerned about their little girl's croup, you can't expect them to think about ordinary things like addresses and telephone numbers. They're very upset. It really isn't very nice of you," she scolded gently, "to be questioning them at a time like this, especially when Samuel Grant III just explained to you what happened with the car."

Susannah almost laughed aloud. It was so like Kate to use Sam's full name when she knew it would be useful. A casual reminder of just exactly who the police were dealing with here.

Kate shot a look of scorn in Callie's direction. "Miss Matthews is hysterical. She gets that way sometimes."

"I do not!" Callie's eyes darted around the room from person to person, desperately seeking assistance. She wanted out of the hole she'd dug for herself.

Jonah Izbecki returned his attention to his patient.

Lily Dolan busied herself with Joanie Sloan's chart.

No one in the room was the slightest bit interested in Callie's plight.

Her face flooded with red again. "I . . . I . . ."

The policeman with the notebook closed it and returned it to his pocket. "No car theft,"

215

he said, turning around, "and no vagrancy. So what are we doing here?" As he joined his partner in the doorway, he said to Callie, his voice cool, "You oughta watch what you tell the police, miss, especially on a night like this one. We got our hands full already with legitimate calls." He signaled to his partner, and they left.

Fuming, Callie was still standing there when Abby came running down the corridor.

"Callie, what are you doing here? I thought you and your dad were going home. I guess you got stuck because of the weather, hmm?" Without waiting for an answer, she bounded into the room and ran over to the bed to give Annie a vigorous hug.

When she let go and straightened up, she grinned happily and cried, "We found Sid! He's downstairs under a warming blanket, but thanks to Damon . . . *and* me, of course . . . he's going to be okay. Isn't that just too perfect?"

Callie turned in disgust and hurried away.

epilogue

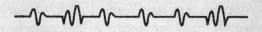

The air was cool and fresh, the sky clear and cloudless as only an early April sky can be. The trees overhead on the grounds of Med Center were just beginning to bud.

"Funny color, that sky," Sam commented. "Sort of a robin's-egg blue. Looks like the same color as Callie's car to me."

Everyone laughed, remembering Callie's tantrum in Joanie Sloan's room the night of the blizzard.

They were sitting on a blanket on the lawn outside of the Rehab building, enjoying the sun and the unusually balmy temperature. All around them, nurses and nurses' aides and orderlies pushed wheelchairs along the pathways. Patients in the chairs lifted their faces to the warm sun. A few of the flowers in the well-manicured beds scattered about the grounds boasted pink or yellow buds that nodded in the gentle breeze.

"Callie acts like none of it ever happened," Susannah said, leaning against Will's chest. "I see her in the halls and she just says hi and struts on her way."

"That," Kate said firmly, "is because you fixed her up with that intern, Alec what's-his-name. She's on cloud nine."

"Alec Blackstone. Yeah, I did." Susannah smiled. "I consider it part of her punishment for being such a brat. I figured they were perfect for each other. They can spend hours talking about their favorite things . . . themselves. Then he'll get bored and dump her."

"That wasn't very nice of you, Susannah," Abby said with mock sternness. She was sitting on Sid's lap in the wheelchair, her arms around his neck. "You know she's going to get her heart broken."

"I only hope I'm around to see it," Lily, sprawled beside Sam on the blanket, said. "The way she acted that night was disgusting. The only thing the Sloans were guilty of was not having a home."

"Yeah, well, that's history," Damon offered. "They're okay now. It must have killed Matthews when she found out her own daddy gave Sloan a job at the lab. I wish I could have seen the look on her face when she heard."

"He didn't do it on his own," Kate reminded him. "Susannah won't admit it, but I know perfectly well her father made Matthews give Sloan a job, one where he'd be sitting down all the time. Easier on his legs that way. I talked to Mrs. Sloan yesterday. They're going to be moving soon, into a rental house in their old neighborhood. She sounded really happy. She wants us all to come to a housewarming party when they get settled. I said we'd be there with bells on, right?"

"Right!"

Jeremy Barlow, fully recovered from the flu, said mournfully, "Sounds to me like I missed a lot of excitement." He was lying on his back on the blanket, hoping an early tan would erase the paleness left by the flu.

"Oh, it was exciting, all right," Susannah answered. "Roads closed, ambulances pouring into the ER, the Sloans nearly getting arrested, not to mention Sam. And then there was Lily's father . . ." Wondering if she'd spoken out of turn, she glanced quickly at Lily.

"It's okay," Lily said. "And by the way, I'm moving, too." She glanced up at Abby and smiled. "O'Connor's family has an apartment over their garage. I'm taking it over. Abby insisted, and I didn't argue. I'm paying a disgustingly low rent, so I can afford it."

"We weren't using it, anyway," Abby said. "My grandfather lived in it once, but then he got too absentminded to live there alone, so he moved in with us. The apartment's been empty ever since. You're really doing us a favor, Lily. We needed someone in there to take care of it."

Lily laughed. "Yeah, right."

"What does your dad think about it?" Susannah asked. She had visions of Tommy Dolan harassing the O'Connor family, a thought that made her very unhappy and anxious.

Lily shrugged. "He'll get over it." She glanced affectionately at Sam. "He's holding onto his temper these days. I think he's afraid he'll lose his job at the refinery if he hits me again and Sam finds out. No job, no money for booze, so it's hands off for now. But I'm still leaving. It's time for me to be out on my own. In the meantime, it's nice having Sam for a friend."

Susannah saw Sam wince at the word "friend." But Lily didn't let go of his hand.

In spite of Sam's obvious disappointment, Susannah thought, Lily is good for him. She's taking her time, not falling all over him like the other girls in town do. It won't hurt him to discover that girls can be friends. It might even make it easier for *me* to talk to him. And I think I'd like that, Susannah thought, smiling.